FRAMED

FRAMED

By Amethyst Drake

For Mom ~
The person who taught
me to love mysteries.

Prologue

Beth walked out of the Cut Right Salon with a spring in her step. Her usual stylist was on vacation, but the owner had given her personal attention. And she felt great.

She looked at herself in her car's vanity mirror. Placing her hand on her stomach, she smiled smugly. Good news from the doctor too.

Beth pulled away from the strip mall and headed east on Fredrick Avenue. The street lamps had begun to glow and traffic thinned as people found their way home. But not Beth. She had more business to attend to this evening.

The Walters Art Museum was dark when she arrived. Beth was surprised to see Misty Vanderlin's car in the lot. A flash of envy threatened to ruin Beth's good mood. Misty had it all. Her own parking space. Curator at the Walters. Respect in the community. A wealthy husband.

A loud beeping drew Beth's attention. Misty was running across the parking lot toward her car. She jumped in and pulled away immediately. Beth smiled. She enjoyed seeing her boss upset. She placed both hands on her stomach and took a deep breath. She was going to give James the one thing his wife couldn't.

Primping her brown hair one last time, Beth stepped into the cold evening air and rounded the corner to the museum's employee entrance. Dim security lights guided her through the breakroom and the main exhibit halls. She finally arrived at a heavy wooden door at the back of the museum's small Neoclassical exhibit.

The door had been closed for weeks as a new exhibit was being set up. The official unveiling for museum patrons was still a week away. Beth had hoped to be the one to show it to James, but of course, Misty had beaten her to it. Beth took a deep breath as she found the large key required to open the old-fashioned lock. She was surprised her lover wasn't already there waiting for her. Misty wouldn't be James's wife much longer, not if Beth had anything to say about it.

The door slid into the wall with a groan and Beth stepped into the room. A glass ceiling arched twenty feet high, letting in a gentle moonlit glow. The walls around the room were lined with Baroque portraits. Beth reached to her left to raise the lights and get a better look at the exhibit she had helped assemble.

A partial wall in the middle of the room held the centerpiece of the collection, a striking 17th century oil on canvas, Judith Decapitating Holofernes. The wall had been painted a deep green to accentuate the large painting's dark shadows, flickering candlelight, and dramatic content. Under the painting, an Italian table from the Baroque Era supported a small bronze statuette depicting Prometheus chained to a rock. But Beth's attention was drawn to the item at the bottom of the display. Wedged under the table in an unnatural position, the body of James Vanderlin, surrounded by a pool of his own blood.

1

"I didn't kill my husband."

The words echoed through Katherine Carson's mind as she navigated the icy Baltimore streets. Monday morning traffic crawled through the freshly fallen snow, giving her too much time to replay Saturday's jailhouse interview with Misty Vanderlin.

"How was your relationship with your husband?"

"Good! I didn't have any reason to kill him."

Three days had passed since the body of James Vanderlin was discovered in the Walters Art Museum's newest exhibit. Police had arrested his wife at the scene. She called her old college roommate, Margaret Mitchell.

"Misty didn't do this, Kat. I've known her for twenty years. She's loyal, honest, and incapable of violence."

Margaret was one of the best criminal defense attorneys in the city. And Katherine's friend since childhood. When Margaret asked her to take on the investigation for the defense, Katherine couldn't say no.

Even though she was far from convinced of their client's innocence.

Driving to the crime scene for her first real look at where it all happened, she couldn't stop analyzing every detail from her conversation with Mrs. Vanderlin.

"What were you doing during the day on Friday?"

"I had some packages arrive. I spent nearly the whole day in the shipping department."

The story itself seemed straightforward enough. The art curator turned murder suspect claimed she was working late Friday night, finalizing paperwork for a new acquisition. A normal day, a normal evening until James texted that he was at the back door.

We need to look into those texts, Katherine thought as she braked at a red light. Mrs. Vanderlin's cell phone records showed she sent James a text at lunch time asking him to come to the museum. "Luring him to his fate," the prosecutor would claim. Their client swore she didn't send the text, and didn't expect James at the museum that evening.

But she let him in and took him to see the new exhibit. She left the exhibit hall for a few minutes to finish repacking a shipping crate before coming back.

"When I went in ... I saw James. Blood on the floor. I couldn't believe it."

What she did next nagged at Katherine as she turned onto Charles Street. Misty Vanderlin had turned off the lights. Locked the door. Driven away. Left her husband's body alone in that dark room.

"I was afraid," Misty had said, tears welling in her eyes. "I was worried what people would think. I just needed time to think."

Katherine had seen genuine trauma before. She'd also seen calculated performances. The problem was, sometimes they looked identical.

The Walters Art Museum came into view, an imposing structure against the gray winter sky. Katherine pulled into the parking lot, finding a spot near the employee entrance where James had entered Friday evening. She turned off the engine but remained in the car, staring at the building.

"I couldn't process what I was seeing. I thought I had time. I was going to call the police when I came back."

But she didn't have time. And she didn't call the police. A witness arriving late at the museum had seen Misty drive away, found the body, and called 911. When Misty did come back, police had already processed the scene and found the security footage that led to her arrest. Lee and Sammi would be at police headquarters right now, reviewing that security footage.

Then there was the gun. Misty owned one, usually kept locked in their home safe. James had insisted on it after a break-in. The police found it at the scene covered in her fingerprints. Only Misty and James had the safe combination. Katherine watched her breath fog the car window as she considered the implications. If Misty was telling the truth, someone had gained access to her phone, her gun, and her safe combination. Someone who knew James well enough to lure him to the museum. Someone with intimate knowledge of the Vanderlin household.

Margaret's faith in her college friend was absolute, but Katherine couldn't afford such certainty. She'd agreed to help investigate, but that meant following the evidence wherever it led, even if it led straight back to their client.

The wind picked up, and her partner Jake Mercer parked his Jeep at the curb. Katherine pulled her coat tighter and grabbed her notebook. Her team had appointments lined up with James's business partner, Owen Lacroix, and his executive assistant,

Anna Bovill. Maybe a business associate was nursing a grudge against the Vanderlins. They needed to piece together James movements, and Misty's, on his last day alive. But first she wanted to see the crime scene with her own eyes. She wanted to walk through the exhibit hall, to stand where Misty claimed she'd found her husband's body, to understand how someone could discover such a scene and respond by turning off lights and locking doors.

As she stepped out into the cold morning air, Katherine's boots crunched on the snow-covered pavement. The same entrance James had used Friday evening loomed ahead of her.

She thought again of Misty's trembling hands, of Margaret's protective concern, of the blood on the museum floor that had started this whole nightmare.

"I didn't kill my husband."

The words followed Katherine as she walked toward the museum, but she pushed them aside. In her experience, the truth was rarely as simple as what people claimed in sterile interview rooms. And sometimes, the people who seemed most desperate to be believed were the ones with the most to hide.

The bus lurched forward as it rattled down Baltimore's uneven streets. Outside, the winter world blurred past as the morning sun overpowered the streetlamps. Sammi sat on the edge of her seat, buzzing with energy. She clasped her hands in her lap, trying to hold in her enthusiasm. She glanced at Lee, who flashed her a wide smile.

"Excited for your first visit to Police Headquarters?" he asked.

Sammi bit her lip. She wanted so much to stay calm and professional.

Lee chuckled softly. "It's okay to be excited. You're finally getting a chance to get out of the office and start learning the ropes."

As the newest member of the Carson Investigations team—okay, fine, technically the administrative assistant for now—Sammi was dying to impress Katherine, Jake, and Lee who had decades of experience in the field. She relaxed into a smile. "I'm so excited, I think I might burst. I'm going to a real live police station to work! Que chévere es eso!"

Even as she said it, a tiny voice in her head whispered that they'd be looking through someone's private pain. She pushed the thought away. This was about finding the truth, right?

Lee grinned. "It's not as cool as they make it seem on TV. No perfect lighting, no dramatic music building up to the big reveal. It's a lot of boring paperwork, interviews, and hours of going through video footage."

Sammi was more curious than disappointed. "You mean it's all about the details, right? Like, looking for clues that no one else can see? That's what I want to do—find the tiny details that tell the whole story."

Lee pointed outside at the city landscape. "That's exactly it. It's about observing what's in front of you, and using what you already know to connect the dots."

"I'm so ready," Sammi said, bouncing in her seat. "I've been watching crime shows since I was a kid, so I've got down the basics. You know, how to spot the lying suspects, how to pick up on the small things that might seem irrelevant ..." Though she wondered if real people's secrets would feel as clean and obvious as they did on TV.

"You're gonna find out fast that it's not as simple as it looks. People will lie about anything. And sometimes, the truth is right there staring you in the face, but you're too focused on the wrong thing."

"So, it's not just about being smart?"

"Nope." Lee stretched out his long legs. "It's about patience. And gut instinct. Sometimes, your brain will tell you one thing. But trust your gut. If it says 'this is wrong' or 'something doesn't add up,' it's right."

Sammi was quiet for a moment, staring at Lee as she absorbed his words. "That sounds ... complicated."

"You want to be a detective, right?" Lee looked at her with a smirk. "This is the real deal. It's messy. It's complicated. And sometimes, you'll feel like you're chasing your tail. But when you catch the bad guy or uncover the truth? There's no better feeling."

"Okay, that's why I'm in this. I want that feeling." Sammi beamed.

The bus pulled up to the station, and Sammi jumped up almost immediately. As they stepped off the bus, she craned her neck to look at the massive building.

"Wow," she gasped in awe, her eyes wide as they entered through the glass doors. "This place is ... huge."

"Welcome to the real world." Lee gave her a knowing smile. "Just wait until you see the conference room. You're about to get a crash course in video analysis."

2

Katherine met Jake at the employee entrance to the Walters Art Museum. "It's been forever since I've been here," she said.

"And I bet you've never come in through the break room," Jake remarked, as they took the same path as James Vanderlin on the night he died. "You should come more often. You've always loved art."

The marble staircase echoed their footsteps as they climbed. Her lips curved up as they entered the Hall of Statues. "I do love art." Katherine's deep blue eyes traced the cold marble gazes that had withstood centuries. She smiled, thinking of Jake. He had been an immovable presence in her life since she was nine years old.

At the top of the stairs, a uniformed officer checked their IDs. He gestured toward the Neo-Classical exhibit. "Detective Eden is expecting you. Just through there."

They followed his directions, stepping into a room with navy walls and framed artwork. A tall black woman in a business suit stood near the back, studying a small painting.

"Rhonda," Katherine called out, her voice carrying across the hushed gallery.

The police detective turned and a quick smile spread across her face. "Right on time, as always, hon. Good to see you both." Her Baltimore accent added warmth to her professional tone. "Though I was hoping not to see you again so soon after the Hannity mess last month. You're taking on one hell of a challenge with the Vanderlin defense."

"Well, we never did like the easy ones." Jake smiled as he shook her hand.

Rhonda smirked. "This isn't just difficult—the evidence is rock solid. Gun at the scene, prints on the murder weapon, documented access to the security systems. You're gonna need more than Margaret Mitchell's silver tongue to get Mrs. Vanderlin out of this." She nodded toward a sliding wooden door. "The scene's back here."

"You caught your suspect fast," Jake observed. He tapped his fingers on his thigh as he scanned the room. Katherine knew his NSA-trained instincts would catalogue every detail.

"Sometimes the perp falls right into your lap, sometimes you gotta chase 'em to kingdom come." Rhonda followed them through the door. "This one might've been too easy. See for yourself."

The gallery was eerily quiet. The glass ceiling arched high above them. Baroque portraits hung on every wall. The Walters was closed on Mondays, so no music was playing and no sounds came from the other galleries. Katherine observed the forensic markers around the room and a faint metallic scent lingering in the air. She took a deep breath, then looked back to Rhonda.

"Here," Rhonda said, walking toward the green-painted partial wall in the center of the room. A stark white outline of a body was taped on the floor. "The deceased was pushed under this table."

"A dramatic backdrop for a murder," Jake said.

Katherine studied the violent imagery in the painting that hung above where James Vanderlin's body was found. A serene Judith pressing the general's own sword through his neck. "I imagine our victim was as surprised as Holofernes." She paused, thinking about connections. "The killer chose this spot deliberately. This is too dramatic to be a coincidence."

Rhonda crossed her arms. "Ten-four on that, hon. We thought the same thing, but can't link the scene to Vanderlin or his wife in any meaningful way. Other than the gallery opening this weekend and Mrs. Vanderlin's role as curator." She handed Katherine a folder and pointed out a few of the evidence markers. "Your client's fingerprints were all over the room."

"She works here," Katherine said, flipping through the folder.

"The murder weapon was registered in her name," Rhonda countered.

Jake crouched beside the taped outline. "Where did you find the gun?"

"Marker three." Rhonda pointed to a spot a few feet outside the tape outline. "A Glock 19. Prints of both Mr. and Mrs. Vanderlin were found on it. It's apparently one of a pair they own. And the shell casing was found here." She walked a few steps back to marker number two.

"Only one?" Jake asked.

"That's right. One shot to the head."

Katherine paused to look at a photo of the body. The victim had been awkwardly shoved under the table at the base of the wall. "Are you confident you've got the right person? Could such a slight woman have moved her husband's body like that?"

Rhonda hesitated, folding her arms. "Well, you know better than most what people are capable of when their adrenaline is racing. The evidence says we have the murderer in custody. Her gun, her presence at the crime scene, her relationship to the victim. But ..." She glanced around as if checking for listeners.

Jake stood and stepped closer to the two women.

"You don't buy it?" Katherine said in a low voice.

"When I questioned Mrs. Vanderlin, she didn't read like a murderer." Rhonda spread out her hands. "She was distraught, sure, but not in the 'I'm faking grief' way. More like she was in shock. Still, evidence doesn't lie."

"And people do," Jake added.

Rhonda nodded. "Exactly. Maybe she's a really good liar. But so far, we haven't found a good motive. By all accounts, they were the picture-perfect power couple. James Vanderlin was charming, successful, loved by everyone."

"Except by whoever shot him." Jake said. He pointed to the bronze statuette of Prometheus on the table above the body outline. "And this? No signs of disturbance?"

"It may have moved slightly, but we can't tell," Rhonda said. "CSU went over the table and the statue with a fine-tooth comb. A few fingerprints, but no evidence of blood or tissue transfer."

"I bet the museum was thrilled about that." Katherine chuckled.

"The assistant curator, Beth Taylor, stood over them the whole time."

"Someone called her?"

"She's the one who found the body."

Katherine noted Beth Taylor's address before returning the file to Rhonda. "Does she know what happened?"

"Sure does, hon. She saw your client running out of the museum and speeding away in her car. Just minutes later, she found him."

Jake had moved to the gallery's door. "Was this lock tampered with?" He leaned closer to examine the door frame and both sides of the old-fashioned lock.

"No." Rhonda shook her head as she moved to door. "No scratches or damage. And it was locked when Ms. Taylor came to check on the exhibit."

Katherine put her hands on her hips. "Let me guess, our client is one of the only people to have a key."

"You got it, hon. Mrs. Vanderlin, Ms. Taylor, and the chief of security." Rhonda pulled the door closed. "And then there's the matter of the security footage. I haven't seen it yet myself, but I understand that it seals the case."

"Alright, well, thanks for the tour." Katherine and Jake left as the police officers resealed the crime scene.

The partners discussed strategy as they exited the museum. Between the crime scene and Misty's interview, they had multiple leads to track down. They finished dividing up the work by the time they reached the parking area.

"I'm going to take Sammi with me to interview the woman who found the body," Katherine said, opening the door of her Ford Focus.

"That'll be good experience for her." Jake zipped his coat against a sudden burst of wind. "You know, if our client's been framed, the killer wanted this to scream her name."

"And if she's guilty?" Katherine asked.

Jake furrowed his brow. "What's your gut telling you?"

"My gut says Misty Vanderlin knows more than she's letting on."

3

"We appreciate this, Sergeant," Lee said, his Southern drawl deepening with deliberate charm.

Sergeant Mendoza huffed. "Everything you need is queued up. The timestamp corresponds to visitor logs." He tapped his watch. "I've got a briefing in thirty, so make it quick."

"We'll be careful with your evidence," Lee replied.

The door closed with a definitive click.

Sammi pulled a chair closer to the dated computer monitor. "They've already decided Mrs. Vanderlin is guilty, haven't they?"

Lee tapped at the keyboard. "That's why we're here. Our client's guilt is the easy answer. We're looking for the right one." He pointed to the screen. "Now, video analysis is all about patterns and anomalies. You watch for what's there and what's not."

He clicked through several feeds showing different museum sections. The next camera angle showed a woman in her forties, moving with purpose toward a side entrance.

"That's her?" Sammi leaned closer.

"Mrs. Misty Vanderlin herself," Lee confirmed. "Museum curator, accused murderer, and our client." He tapped a key, adjusting the speed. "Watch her body language. She's comfortable, familiar with the space."

The woman reached the door, glanced around, then opened it. A tall man in a dark suit entered.

"James Vanderlin."

Sammi chewed her lip. "She doesn't look nervous about sneaking him in."

"She's not sneaking. Her job gives her full access." Lee stretched his arms over his head. "The prosecution could say bringing him to an empty museum shows premeditation. I say it shows a wife giving her husband a private tour."

They watched as the couple moved through the museum corridors. Mrs. Vanderlin gestured occasionally, pointing out items as they walked. Both figures appeared to be smiling the whole time.

"Camera three, camera five, camera eight." Lee counted as they passed each camera.

"Wait, pause it," Sammi said suddenly. "Go back." Her finger jabbed toward the screen. "There! When they pass that statue. Did you see that?"

Lee rewound the footage. "Good catch. Whatcha see?"

"Their reflection in the glass display case. Mrs. Vanderlin is holding his arm, like, super close. They look ... happy?" Sammi looked up at Lee. "Not exactly the vibe you'd expect from someone about to commit murder, right?"

"That's an excellent observation. We document everything, especially things that contradict the official narrative."

The footage continued. The couple approached a set of double doors marked "Baroque Gallery, Opening Next Week."

"Now it gets interesting," Lee said, slowing the playback. "Camera nine shows them entering the restricted exhibit."

Mrs. Vanderlin produced a key and unlocked the large doors. They entered together.

"Camera twelve is inside the gallery." Lee referenced his notes.

The new angle showed the couple moving through the sealed exhibit. In the center, dramatically lit, hung a massive oil painting in an ornate gold frame. They watched as James Vanderlin approached the painting, becoming utterly still before it. Mrs. Vanderlin spoke to him briefly, then checked her watch and gestured toward a door at the rear of the gallery.

"She's leaving him there?" Sammi asked.

"Heading to the storage room," Lee confirmed. "No cameras there. It's a blind spot."

On screen, James remained transfixed by the painting, barely moving.

Lee sped up the playback. "Time stamp shows he's been staring at that painting for almost three minutes."

Sammi shook her head. "That's some serious art appreciation."

Suddenly, the feed from camera twelve flickered, distorted, and went black.

With a couple keystrokes, Lee reversed the footage and reset the playback speed. Sure enough, one moment the image showed James Vanderlin staring at a painting. The next moment, the camera went out.

"And we're offline," Lee grumbled, his voice dropping. "Convenient timing."

Sammi straightened. "Can we recover any of that?"

"System registers it as a complete outage. Camera twelve goes down at 8:41 PM. Three minutes after Mrs. Vanderlin left the room at 8:38 PM." Lee switched to another feed. "We can still see the door outside on camera nine. These Nuvico systems operate on separate circuits—when one camera fails, the others stay online."

A few minutes passed on the timestamp. Suddenly, Mrs. Vanderlin emerged from the gallery, her movements hurried. She fumbled with her keys, locking the doors behind her.

"Look at her face," Sammi whispered. "She looks terrified."

"Running scared," Lee agreed.

The footage showed Mrs. Vanderlin rushing through the museum and out the same side entrance she'd used earlier.

"Time check—8:46 PM," Lee noted. "Five minutes after the camera failure."

The next sequence showed a younger woman entering the museum through the side door at 8:49 PM. She walked directly to the Baroque gallery.

"Beth Taylor, assistant curator," Lee explained. "Working late, according to her statement."

They watched as she unlocked the gallery doors and stepped inside. A few minutes later, she came running out, phone pressed to her ear, her free hand waving wildly.

"The 911 call was logged at 8:55 PM." Lee stopped the playback. "Police arrived at 9:02. Found James Vanderlin dead from a single gunshot wound to the head."

Sammi slumped back in her chair. "This looks bad for our client, doesn't it? Really bad. She had access, opportunity, and there's literally video of her running from the scene of the crime."

Lee's eyes crinkled at the corners. "Here's what the police are seeing: wife brings husband to empty museum, leads him to a secluded gallery, disables the camera, shoots him, then flees. Open and shut."

"Isn't it?" Sammi asked, deflated.

"Maybe." Lee rewound the footage again. "But here's what I'm seeing: no sign of conflict between the couple, no weapon visible at any point, and Mrs. Vanderlin leaves the room before the camera fails."

"But she could have planned it that way," Sammi countered.

"Could have," Lee agreed. "But why would she run out the same door she came in, knowing she'd be on camera? Why not use the service corridors that are not monitored?"

Sammi straightened in her chair. "You think someone else could have been there?"

"I think we need all the facts before jumping to conclusions. That's how mistakes are made." Lee knew all too well how assumptions and false conclusions could derail an operation. He'd witnessed it first hand during his time at the NSA. He tapped a few keys, saving the security footage to a portable drive. "The camera failure is too convenient. This system is pretty reliable. Wiring issue, maybe, but more likely someone tampered with it."

"The storage room has no cameras," Sammi said slowly. "Someone could have been hiding there, waiting."

"Now you're thinking like a detective." Lee shot her a lopsided grin of approval. "Don't let what you expect to see blind you to what's actually there. Or in this case, what's not there."

Sammi's eyes lit up. "We should check if anyone else was still in the museum that night! And we need to see if the wiring to camera twelve was cut or something."

"That's the spirit." Lee pocketed the drive with a copy of the footage. "But remember, evidence is like a jigsaw puzzle. Some pieces face down, some face up, and a few might belong to a different puzzle altogether."

"So we keep looking until the picture makes sense," Sammi said with determination.

Katherine parked her car outside Baltimore Police Head-quarters to wait for Sammi and Lee. A rare moment of stillness in the middle of an investigation. She glanced at her watch. Her mind drifted back to her interview with their client that morning.

The break-in at the Vanderlin home last year.

The purchase of two guns.

James teaching his wife to shoot.

The feeling of becoming a widow.

Another husband trying to protect his wife through weapons training. Her thoughts shifted to Daniel and their shared past at the Espionage Services Agency. She'd been born into that world—a third-generation secret agent. Daniel had been recruited from Yale University. Brilliant, but playing catch-up in a game she'd trained for since childhood.

She felt the weight of her knife in her pocket. Her weapon of choice, despite Daniel's protests. Two-point five inches of purpose, of control. She opened the Ridge Summit and turned it over, appreciating the black, high carbon blade.

Not as lethal as the 4.5-inch extension of herself that she used to carry.

But it would do. It always had.

"A knife. You were relying on a knife?" Daniel Carson's voice quavered with disbelief.

"I just took down two armed men!" A young Katherine retorted playfully.

"In a training scenario." Daniel's tactical vest was dusty from the morning exercise. A smudge of paint lingered on his temple.

Katherine spun her ESEE-4 between her fingers, a movement practiced to perfection. "My father gave me my first blade when I was five." She sheathed it behind her neck in a swift, elegant motion. "Some tools become part of you."

Daniel checked the magazine on his Sig Sauer before holstering it. "And some tools keep you alive when the other guy has superior firepower." His movements were the textbook perfect result of intensive training rather than a lifetime of practice.

Katherine smirked. "I've killed with knives on three continents. Seems effective to me."

"The Juárez mission next month won't leave room for sentimentality. The Agency has protocols for a reason, Kate." Daniel crossed his arms.

"Listen, Yale." Katherine raised an eyebrow. "My parents were running operations before you knew what the acronym ESA stood for. And my name is Katherine. Kat to my friends."

Daniel stepped closer, his blue-gray eyes searching hers with intensity. "Okay, Kat. Let me teach you to shoot."

Katherine's hair stood on end at the proximity and the presumption. "I prefer my knife."

A sharp rap on the car window jerked Katherine back to the present. She instinctively gripped her knife tighter before recognizing Sammi's face peering through the foggy glass.

Katherine slipped the blade back into her pocket and lowered the window.

"Sorry we're late," Sammi said, with no hint of remorse. "You're gonna flip when you see what we found!"

"The video footage?" Katherine asked, pushing back her memories.

Sammi yanked open the passenger door, practically bouncing as she slid into the seat. Lee followed at a more measured pace, folding his lanky frame into the back.

"The security camera in the Baroque Gallery went offline at exactly 8:41 PM—just minutes before the murder must have happened. That's way too convenient to be a coincidence!" Sammi clicked her seat belt into place. "There's a blind spot in the security system—the storage room has no cameras at all. Someone could have been hiding there the whole time!"

Katherine smiled at Sammi's exuberance. "Good work. Does the footage show the arrival of the witness?"

Lee answered, "We have video of when Beth Taylor entered the room, and when she left. But nothing from inside the gallery after the camera failure."

"And guess what!" Sammi interjected. "Beth was in the gallery with James, or with his body, for nearly five minutes before she called 911. Isn't that odd?"

"Well," Katherine said, "it's a good thing that our next stop is an interview with Miss Taylor."

4

Katherine parked the car across from Beth Taylor's apartment building. "Remember, in interviews like this, what they don't say is often more important than what they do say."

Sammi twisted a strand of long brown hair around her finger. "I've been reviewing my textbook on the Reid technique. Should I take notes on her body language too?"

"Yes, but discreetly. We want her comfortable enough to talk." Katherine turned to face her apprentice. "This woman has either witnessed a murder or committed one. Either way, she's in shock, even if she doesn't show it."

"She certainly looked upset on the security video from the museum. But she was in the room with the body for five minutes! Long enough to leave clues or to hide evidence."

"Let's not jump to conclusions," Katherine cautioned, though she was pleased by Sammi's insight. "Remember what I told you about first impressions?"

"They're invaluable but need verification," Sammi recited, then added with a self-deprecating smile, "and my excitement about being right often clouds my judgment."

Katherine smiled. "You're learning. Now, if I signal you like this," she tapped two fingers against her knee, "it means let me handle the next question. Not because your questions aren't good—"

"But because timing matters," Sammi finished. "I know. I promise I won't get carried away."

The scent of vanilla and old wood hit Katherine as soon as the door opened. At her side, Sammi practically vibrated with nervous energy. Katherine gave her a steadying look as they followed Beth into her cozy apartment. Soft lighting filled the room, casting a warm glow on cream walls adorned with framed art prints.

Katherine immediately recognized Klimt, Monet, and Matisse reproductions. "You have a beautiful collection," she said, nodding toward the wall.

Behind her, Sammi pulled out her notepad with such enthusiasm that Katherine had to suppress a grin.

Beth's brown eyes flicked between them. "I like to surround myself with beauty. Please, make yourselves comfortable."

Katherine took a seat on the sleek gray couch. Sammi perched beside her with perfect posture, pencil poised. Beth settled gracefully into the armchair opposite them, smoothing her skirt over her long legs.

Katherine began, "Let's start with the basics. What brought you to the museum the night of the incident?"

"I had some appointments that afternoon. The salon, the doctor ..." Beth placed her hand on her stomach. "Then I went to the Walters. When I pulled into the lot, I saw Misty's car. Her private spot, of course." A shadow crossed her face. "Then she came running out, looking completely unhinged. She just jumped in her car and sped away."

"What happened next?" Sammi asked.

"I went into the museum to check on the new exhibit."

"The door was locked?" Sammi wrote furiously in her notebook.

"That's right. I used my key to unlock the door. The room was dark except for the moonlight coming through the glass ceiling. I remember thinking how beautiful it looked, how perfect it would be for me to tell James ..." She swallowed hard. "I reached for the light switch on my left. That's when I saw him."

Katherine tapped her knee with two fingers, giving Beth space to keep talking.

Beth twisted at the fabric of her skirt. "He was wedged under the Italian table, the one beneath the Judith painting. The irony of that ..." She gave a brittle laugh. "I thought maybe he'd fallen at first, but then why was he wedged under that table?"

Katherine noticed that Beth's voice was steady as she described the gruesome scene. "What did you do?"

"I screamed. The sound echoed off the walls. Then I called the police."

"According to security footage, you were in the room with the body for five minutes before you called 911." Katherine felt her apprentice leaning forward beside her, engrossed in the story.

Beth stood suddenly, moving to adjust one of her prints that wasn't crooked. "I didn't touch him. I just stood there, staring. The blood was spreading across the floor. My shoes were new."

Katherine motioned for Sammi to keep taking notes.

Beth spoke in a faraway voice, "All that blood on the floor, looking almost black in the dim light. I remember the bronze

Prometheus statue on the table above him was off-center. I wanted to fix it, isn't that strange? My hands were shaking so badly I could barely get my phone out to call 911." She spun back toward the detectives. "Did you say security footage?"

Sammi answered with a little too much excitement. "Yes, from the new security system! There is a camera clearly showing the door to the Baroque Gallery."

"And inside?"

"No," Katherine stated, "the camera inside the gallery had failed."

A smile or a smirk tugged at Beth's mouth. Katherine couldn't tell which.

Beth dropped back into the chair. "The police said he'd been shot. How could she do that to him?"

"You sound certain she killed him," Katherine observed.

"Of course she killed him. She practically ran to her car." Beth's face hardened. "I've never seen her so undone. The perfect curator, always so composed, but that night ... She couldn't handle losing him. Losing control."

"What do you mean, 'losing him'?" Sammi's pencil paused above the notebook.

"James was leaving her. For me." Beth's voice caught.

Katherine heard Sammi gasp and shot her apprentice a look of warning.

Beth chuckled. "That's right. James and I were lovers."

Katherine kept her own expression neutral, though her stomach clenched. Misty Vanderlin had said her marriage was good. She never mentioned an affair. "How long were you together?"

"Six months."

Katherine's eyebrows lifted. "And you told the police about this relationship?"

Beth's face flushed. "No, not yet. But I will. Unless you do something to change my mind. I'm sure the police would be happy to learn about Misty's motive for killing her husband." Her voice grew sharper with each word.

Katherine lifted her chin. "I'm sure they would also be interested in knowing about your motive to kill your lover. Are you sure he was leaving his wife to be with you?" She placed a gentle hand on Sammi's knee to keep the trainee from fidgeting.

"I know what you're thinking." Beth's tone soured. "You think I'm the other woman with fantasies about stealing the husband away. But he would have left her. He would've had to." Her eyes gleamed with ambition. "I was about to give him something his wife couldn't. A child."

Sammi dropped her pencil. Katherine understood her shock. This case was becoming far more complicated than anyone had expected.

Jake pushed through the heavy glass doors of the Charm City Gun Club. A distinct odor hit him immediately. Gun oil, cordite, and the metallic tang that permeated any well-used range.

The club wasn't flashy, but it had character. Trophy cabinets lined the wood-paneled walls, displaying decades of marksmanship awards beneath soft recessed lighting. Framed black-and-white photos showcased founding members, stern-faced men with revolvers and hunting rifles from another era. Past the reception desk, the muffled pop-pop-pop of someone practicing on the indoor range provided a rhythmic backdrop to the quiet lobby.

"Help ya?" A middle-aged man looked up from behind the counter, reading glasses perched precariously on his nose. He wore a faded green polo shirt with the club's emblem and a tag imprinted with the name "Todd."

Jake flashed his credentials. "I'm Jake Mercer, a private detective. Investigating the murder of James Vanderlin."

Todd's expression shifted from casual to guarded. "Yeah, heard about that on the news. Nasty business."

"I understand the Vanderlins were members here."

"James sure was. Eight, maybe nine years?" Todd turned to a computer terminal. "Started bringing the wife last year. Pretty Hispanic lady. Quiet type."

Jake nodded, studying the range through the viewing window while Todd searched the records. Three shooters were practicing—an elderly man with a revolver, and what looked like a father teaching his teenage son proper stance with a .22.

"Here we go." Todd squinted at the screen. "James Vanderlin, member since 2001. Misty Vanderlin added as a family member February last year. Premium membership—gave them access to the private range upstairs and lockers for their equipment."

"I understand they purchased matching weapons?"

Todd nodded. "Custom Glocks. Pretty pieces—had 'em engraved with their initials. His and hers deal. Anniversary gift, he said."

Jake raised an eyebrow. "Romantic."

"To each their own." Todd shrugged. "She wasn't thrilled with it, though. Totally out of her element here. Only came in two, maybe three times."

"Any records of when they last came in?"

Todd scrolled through the system. "She hasn't been here since April 27. He came in more regular. Last time was ..." He squinted at the screen. "... January 12."

Three days before he was murdered, Jake thought. He moved closer to the counter, watching as Todd pulled up the attendance records. "Was he alone?"

"Nah, he brought a guest that day. Same woman he'd been bringing for months."

"Guest have a name?"

"Just signed in as 'guest'. That's normal procedure for members bringing someone." Todd scratched his neck. "Started bringing her maybe six months back. Said she was his assistant, needed to learn for personal protection."

Jake maintained his neutral expression, though his interest had sharpened. "This assistant. Can you describe her?"

"Brunette. Tall. Always dressed real nice—business clothes, you know? Professional type."

"How often did they come in?"

"Once a week, usually Thursdays. Late afternoon." Todd leaned forward. "They always used the private range upstairs. More expensive, but soundproofed better and no waiting."

Jake nodded, making mental notes. "How was she as a shooter?"

"Started shaky, most beginners do, but got decent fast. He was patient with her. More patient than he ever seemed with his wife, if I'm honest."

Jake's eyes narrowed slightly. "How so?"

"Just different energy, you know? With the wife, it was all business. With the assistant ..." Todd hummed. "Let's just say he stood closer than needed when showing her how to aim."

Jake let the implication hang while he studied the sign-in records on Todd's screen.

"Any security cameras in the parking lot? Maybe at the entrance?"

Todd shook his head. "Owner's been promising to upgrade, but ... " He gestured vaguely, the universal sign for "cheap boss."

Jake pulled out his phone, tapped a quick message to Lee: "At gun club. Vanderlin brought female 'assistant' here regularly for private lessons. Brunette, tall, professional. Any chance Anna Bovill fits that description?"

The reply came almost immediately: "Interviewing her now. 5'9", dark hair, executive assistant for 12 years."

Jake typed back: "Ask if she owns a firearm."

"Found something?" Todd asked, noticing Jake's focus on his phone.

"Maybe." Jake slipped the phone back into his pocket. "You said they had a private locker?"

"Yeah, upstairs by the premium range."

"I'd like to see it."

As Todd led him toward the stairs, Jake's phone buzzed again. Lee's message was just three words:

"She has two."

5

Lee pressed the doorbell of the well-maintained Baltimore row house, adjusting his scarf against the biting wind.

The door swung open to reveal a woman in her early forties with careful makeup and shrewd eyes. She wore a tailored pantsuit with her brown hair pulled back in a bun.

"Can I help you?" she asked in a tone that suggested she'd rather not.

Lee offered his most disarming smile. "Anna Bovill? I'm Lee Stewart." He held up his ID. "I was hoping to ask you a few questions about James Vanderlin."

"The police already questioned me thoroughly." Each word was methodical. "I have nothing to add."

"I reckon they did," Lee nodded agreeably, "but we're looking at things from a different angle. I'm working with Misty Vanderlin's defense team."

Anna's perfectly shaped eyebrows arched. "Defense team? The police found the murder weapon with her prints all over it. What's there to defend?"

"Just trying to make sure all the facts line up. It'll only take a few minutes of your time. As Mr. Vanderlin's executive assistant, you'd know his schedule better than just about anyone."

A man's voice called from inside. "Who is it, hon?"

Anna hesitated. "A private investigator regarding James."

A stocky man appeared behind her, his hands moving expressively. "Oh! A PI! Let him in, Anna. James deserves justice, and if answering a few questions helps, what's the harm?"

"Thank you kindly, sir." Lee extended his hand as he stepped inside. "Lee Stewart."

"Kyle Bovill," the man replied with an enthusiastic handshake, his words coming rapidly. "Can't believe what happened. Terrible thing, just terrible! You think they arrested the right person? I have my own theories about what might have—"

"Kyle," Anna interjected with quiet authority, "perhaps Mr. Stewart would like to sit down."

The foyer opened into a living room where renovation materials were stacked neatly in one corner, including plastic sheeting and paint cans.

"Pardon the mess," Kyle said, his hands gesturing wildly toward the construction materials. "Bathroom remodel. You know how these things go. Start with one project and suddenly you're knee-deep in plumbing work! But I'm making good progress. Very good progress indeed. Don't you think so, Anna?"

"Kyle's quite the handyman," Anna said, visibly relaxing at the casual conversation.

"No need to apologize. My apartment looks worse on a good day," Lee said with a self-deprecating smile. "Y'all doin' the work yourselves?"

Kyle nodded. "Trying to. Got some new tile being delivered today."

Anna gestured toward the sofa. "Have a seat, Mr. Stewart."

Lee kept up his easy-going act as he settled onto the couch, but inwardly he was wound tight as a spring. He hadn't expected a personal connection between James and his assistant. Yet there it was on the mantel amongst the family photos. Young Anna, James and Kyle in formal wear. A snapshot from their high school days, carefully kept through the years.

"So y'all went to school together?" Lee asked. His voice was casual, but he was carefully observing their reactions.

"Oh yes!" Kyle jumped in before Anna could respond, his hands painting pictures in the air. "All three of us. Class of 1981. James and I were on the football team together. I was the tight end, he was quarterback. And debate club too! I won more debates that he did, but whose counting? We dominated regionals our senior year. Isn't that right, Anna?"

"Yes, dear," Anna replied.

"And homecoming court, right?" Lee pointed to the photo.

"King and queen," Kyle confirmed with a dramatic gesture toward his wife. "James and Anna were the perfect pair back then. The golden couple! Everyone thought they'd end up together, but life has its twists and turns, doesn't it? How did you get involved in this case, anyway? Did Misty hire you directly, or was it through her lawyer?"

Lee noticed how Anna froze at the mention of being James's "perfect pair."

Interesting. Lee addressed Anna directly. "Small world, you ending up working with James."

Anna perched on the edge of her chair as if ready to flee. "I became James's executive assistant when he moved home twelve years ago. He appreciated my organizational skills."

"Must be nice, working with an old friend," Lee said.

"The relationship was strictly professional," Anna clarified, words precise and clipped. "James was my employer, not my companion."

"Now, Anna," Kyle interjected, leaning forward eagerly, "you and James were closer than that. We had him over for dinner all the time. And he was always asking for your input on business decisions, wasn't he? More than just an assistant, if you ask me. More like a partner! Right?"

She shot her husband a look that Lee couldn't quite interpret. "I performed my duties competently. Look, Mr. Stewart," she turned back to him, each word carefully chosen, "I fail to see how this assists Misty's defense. The evidence appears conclusive."

Lee leaned forward. "You're right. I just need to get a complete picture of James's last days. Did anything seem unusual about his behavior recently? Any deviations from his typical patterns?"

Anna paused momentarily, collecting her thoughts. "No. Business meetings, finance committee, calls with our overseas partners. James adhered to regular routines."

"What about the day he died?" Lee asked. "Anything stand out?"

A flicker of emotion crossed Anna's face before she answered with deliberate slowness. "No. Standard operational day."

"Did he mention plans to visit the museum that evening?"

"It wasn't on his calendar. But he received a text message from Misty during the lunch hour. She requested his presence for a preview of the new exhibit."

"Was that typical behavior? Her inviting him to the museum after hours?"

"Such invitations occurred periodically," Anna confirmed. "James consistently supported her professional endeavors."

"They had a good marriage then?" Lee asked, trying to dig deeper.

"James demonstrated complete devotion to her." Anna's tone was neutral, but her right hand gripped the arm of the chair.

"Always talking about her!" Kyle jumped in, his hands moving animatedly. "He hit the jackpot with Misty ... beautiful, smart Latina woman who could have had anyone. Don't you think so, Lee? A real catch! Although—"

Anna shot her husband a sharp look that silenced him immediately. The knuckles on her right hand went white. Lee had to suppress a smile at the interaction. There it was, resentment, plain as day.

The doorbell rang, interrupting the moment.

Kyle leapt to his feet. "Oh! That'll be the delivery. Excuse me a moment. Very important materials coming in. Top quality tiles from Italy. Did you know Italian porcelain has superior durability compared to domestic options? Fascinating manu-facturing process. I can tell you all about it when I get back!"

As Kyle rushed to answer the door, Lee turned his full attention to Anna. "I couldn't help but notice you were close in high school. You and James, I mean."

Anna smoothed invisible wrinkles from her pants. "That relationship concluded approximately two decades ago, Mr. Stewart."

"Call me Lee," he said warmly. "And sure, high school's ancient history, but first loves have a way of leaving an impression."

Her eyes snapped to his. "Are you implying something specific?"

"Not implying anything." Lee raised his hands in a placating gesture. "Just makin' conversation while your husband's occupied."

Anna studied him, folding her hands in her lap. "Yes, James and I were romantically involved during high school. Subsequently, we attended different universities. He met Misty, they established a marriage, conclusion of narrative."

"And you're happy with Kyle."

"Affirmative," Anna said firmly. "James and I maintained a professional relationship. Nothing more."

"Did you and Misty get along?"

A pause, longer than her others, before she answered with precision. "We maintained professional courtesy. She failed to integrate with our established social circle, so interactions outside professional settings were minimal."

"Different interests?"

"Different backgrounds," Anna said. "She was adequately pleasant. James valued her, which was the relevant factor."

The sound of Kyle's rapid-fire speech directing someone toward the back of the house floated in from the foyer. Lee reached for his phone when it buzzed with a text from Jake. "At gun club. Vanderlin brought female 'assistant' here regularly for private lessons."

"So, your husband said you had the Vanderlins over for dinner sometimes?" Lee asked while responding to the text.

"No. Just James. When his wife was working late."

"Mrs. Bovill, do you own any firearms?"

The question clearly caught her off guard. "No. I mean. I don't shoot."

Lee held her gaze silently, anticipating a "but."

Anna sighed. "Kyle owns two handguns. He and James would occasionally go shooting. I have never operated them."

"Never been curious? Never requested instruction?" Lee pressed.

"No." Anna glanced briefly toward the hallway where Kyle had disappeared. "I find firearms objectionable."

Lee nodded thoughtfully. "That's interesting. We have a witness from the Charm City Gun Club who says James was teaching his assistant how to shoot."

The color drained from Anna's face, but before she could respond, Kyle returned to the room.

"Sorry about that!" he said, his words spilling out rapidly, then stopped short at the sight of his wife's expression. "Anna? Is everything alright? What did I miss? Has something happened?"

Lee turned to Kyle with a friendly smile. "I was just asking your wife about her whereabouts last Friday night, when James was killed."

Kyle's animated demeanor shifted instantly. His hands stopped moving, and he stammered, "I ... well ... you see ... the thing is ..." He paused, regaining his composure. "What exactly are you suggesting? Are you implying something about my wife?"

"Just routine questions."

"What about that museum security guard who was fired last month? Have you looked into him?" Kyle demanded.

Anna remained seated, her face a careful mask, but Lee could see how rigidly she held herself.

"I appreciate your time," Lee said, rising unhurriedly from the couch. "I'm sure the gun club manager just got confused about which assistant Mr. Vanderlin was teaching how to operate a pistol."

Something flashed in Kyle's eyes—Surprise? Alarm? He glanced quickly at Anna. "Oh, I'm sure that's it. A simple confusion. These things happen all the time in investigations, don't they? Witnesses getting details mixed up? I've read about that. Fascinating field, criminal investigation. Have you been doing this long? Where did you train?"

"Just one more thing." Lee ignored the attempt to change the subject and paused at the door. "What color is your car, Mrs. Bovill?"

"A silver Audi," she answered automatically, then frowned, her words slowing again. "Why is that relevant?"

Lee smiled. "No particular reason. Thank you both for your hospitality."

"Let me walk you out," Kyle insisted, moving between Lee and Anna.

Kyle practically pushed the detective onto the porch, closing the door firmly behind him.

"Well? First impressions?"

"She's hiding something," Sammi said with confidence. "Did you see how she smiled when you said there was no camera inside the gallery?"

"I did." Katherine signaled to turn at the light. "What else?"

Sammi flipped through her notes. "Her story about finding the body bothered me. All those specific details about the statue being off-center, the blood, her new shoes ... My criminology professor always said that people who 'discover' bodies they've actually killed tend to notice odd details instead of focusing on the victim. And that five-minute delay before calling 911? Textbook composure time."

"Good observations. What about her body language when she mentioned the pregnancy?"

Sammi felt a swell of pride as she exchanged thoughts about the case with her mentor. "Protective. Her hand went to her stomach twice, and her voice changed. That felt genuine."

"So we have a pregnant woman claiming her married lover was about to leave his wife, a wife who insists her marriage was solid, and a dead husband who can't tell us the truth." Katherine drummed her fingers on the steering wheel. "Miss Taylor has motive, whether James was leaving Misty or staying with her."

"You think she killed him?"

"I think we need to verify that pregnancy claim and find out what James Vanderlin was really planning to do." Katherine glanced at her apprentice. "And next time, try not to gasp audibly when a witness drops a bombshell. She was watching your reactions as much as mine."

Sammi flushed, deflated. "Sorry. I'll work on my poker face."

"You're learning. That's what matters."

6

"I appreciate you making time to see me," Jake said as he took a seat in the gleaming financial district office.

Derrick Freeman straightened his already impeccable tie. "Mrs. Vanderlin instructed me to cooperate fully with your investigation. I must say, I find it hard to believe she had anything to do with James's death."

"How would you characterize the Vanderlins' financial situation?"

"Rock solid," Freeman replied, a hint of pride in his voice. "I've managed their portfolio for three years now. No liquidity issues, diversified investments, strong returns." He swiveled his monitor toward Jake. "I can show you their quarterly statements if you'd like."

"I'll take a look," Jake said, studying the screen. "Any unusual activity in the past six months? Large withdrawals, unexpected deposits?"

Freeman shook his head emphatically. "Nothing out of pattern. Their spending is consistent with their lifestyle and income."

"What about regular withdrawals of smaller amounts? Something that might indicate blackmail?"

"No," Freeman said, his brow furrowing. "Nothing that raises flags. They're quite comfortable financially. They own their primary residence outright, plus the summer place in Nantucket and two other investment properties."

Jake leaned back in his chair. "Tell me about the break-in last year."

Surprise flickered across Freeman's face. "You're thorough, Mr. Mercer."

"That's what people pay me for."

"Fair enough. From what they told me, it wasn't a major incident. Some damage to the property, but nothing of significant value was taken. They were out of town when it happened." Freeman hesitated. "It did shake them up, though. James mentioned they'd purchased firearms afterward. Not my area of expertise. Their insurance broker could tell you more."

Jake made a note in his small notebook. "Let's talk about their accounts. Joint or separate?"

"Both." Freeman clicked through screens. "They maintain joint investment accounts and a joint checking account for household expenses. James handled most of the major expenditures—charitable donations, vacations, that sort of thing." He paused. "The Walters Art Museum was a particular focus. Misty works there as a curator, and James served on the board."

"And Misty's personal accounts?"

"She maintained her own checking and savings, funded by her salary and quarterly bonuses from the museum. Modest income compared to James's, but she used it for personal expenses, gifts, entertaining, that sort of thing."

"Did either of them ever express concerns about money? Arguments over spending habits?"

"Never," Freeman replied confidently, then paused. "Mr. Mercer, do you really think Mrs. Vanderlin could have—"

"I don't speculate, Mr. Freeman," Jake cut in. "I gather facts. One more question. Did James ever mention problems at the museum? Conflicts with board members, staff issues, anything like that?"

Freeman's eyes widened slightly. "He did mention some tension over a new acquisition. Said there was disagreement about its authenticity. But that was months ago, and he never brought it up again."

Jake stood, extending his hand. "You've been helpful. If you think of anything else, even something that seems insignificant, call me." He handed Freeman his card.

As Jake drove away from the financial district, he pulled out his phone and pressed a familiar number.

"Katie? It's me. The financial angle looks clean on the surface, but there's scuttlebutt about a disputed artwork at the museum. Might be nothing, but …."

"But your instincts say otherwise," Katherine finished for him. "I may have a lead for us to find out more about that. Meet me at the office in thirty."

Katherine was organizing case files as some welcome sunshine streamed through the office's west-facing windows. The frosted glass door with "CARSON INVESTIGATIONS" stenciled in gold opened with a hesitant creak.

A woman stood in the doorway, clutching her purse tightly. Her eyes were rimmed red, and she looked over her shoulder before stepping inside.

Katherine watched the woman take in the office. Lee hunched over a computer on one side of the room typing reports. Sammi arranging photographs on the corkboard behind Katherine's desk. The woman's gaze finally settled on Katherine herself.

"I'm looking for Ms. Carson? Are you ... available?" she asked. "Dr. Patel upstairs said you might be able to help me."

"That's right," Katherine replied, her pulse quickening. Dr. Nisha Patel, the dentist who occupied the floor above them in the Mt. Vernon Business Center, had sent referrals before. Usually clients who mentioned their troubles while captive in her chair.

"Please, have a seat. This is Sammi Garcia, one of my associates, and that's Lee Stewart over there."

Lee waved without looking up from his screen. "Ma'am."

Sammi stepped forward eagerly. "Can I take your coat?"

The woman was clearly distressed but trying to maintain composure. She handed her coat to Sammi with trembling fingers.

"Coffee?" Katherine asked, gesturing to the small kitchenette.

"Please." The woman nodded. She took a seat on one of the two sofas that served as the agency's informal conference room.

"I'll get that for you," Sammi said, adopting the professional tone Katherine had been teaching her. "How do you take it?"

"Black is fine," the woman replied, her gaze darting around the office.

Katherine sat on the opposite sofa and observed their potential client carefully. Mid-thirties, well-dressed, but not ostentatious. Manicured nails but chewed cuticles. A woman under stress. She caught Sammi's eye and gave her a subtle wink, signaling this would be a teaching moment.

"I'm Katherine Carson," she began. "What brings you to us today, Ms. ...?"

"Hackett. Cynthia Hackett." She accepted the mug from Sammi with a grateful nod. "I need ... discretion."

From his desk, Lee's typing slowed almost imperceptibly. Katherine knew he was listening while pretending not to. A useful habit from his intelligence gathering days.

"Discretion is our specialty, Ms. Hackett," Katherine assured her. "Why don't you tell us what's troubling you?"

Sammi sat on the sofa with Katherine across from Ms. Hackett. Katherine gave her an encouraging nod. This was the perfect opportunity for her apprentice to practice her interview skills.

"What specifically brought you here today?" Sammi asked, her usual enthusiasm tempered into professional interest.

Cynthia Hackett took a shaky breath. "It's my boyfriend, Christopher. He's been ... different lately. Coming into money and won't tell me where it's from." She clutched the coffee mug tighter. "It started several months ago. Cash. Always cash."

"How much money are we talking about?" Katherine laced her fingers together, mentally listing possibilities: gambling, drugs, theft, blackmail.

"A few thousand here and there. Nothing consistent. But it's the secrecy that bothers me." Cynthia placed her mug on the coffee table between them. "And the late-night phone calls he takes in the bathroom with the shower running."

In the corner, Lee's chair creaked as he shifted his weight.

"Have you asked him directly about this?" Sammi asked, her pen poised over the notepad.

"Of course!" Cynthia frowned. "He says it's just 'work stuff' and changes the subject. But he's an accountant. Accountants don't get paid in cash at midnight."

"What exactly are you hoping we can discover, Ms. Hackett?" Katherine asked.

Cynthia looked up. "I need to know if he's involved in something illegal. Or if he's ..." She swallowed hard. "If there's someone else."

Katherine felt a familiar tightness in her chest as the weight of someone else's fears and suspicions transferred to her shoulders. "We can find out what's happening," she stated simply. "But you need to be prepared for whatever that might be."

Beside her, Katherine saw Sammi grow tense. The rookie was still learning the hardest lesson of detective work: not every truth sets you free.

"Sammi, why don't you walk Ms. Hackett through our standard intake process?" she suggested, offering her associate the lead while keeping a watchful eye.

Sammi straightened her shoulders, clearly proud of the responsibility. "Of course. Ms. Hackett, we'll need some basic information to begin our investigation ..."

Katherine walked back to the desk area while Sammi went through some routine questions. She paused when she saw a message from Detective Rhonda Eden on her BlackBerry. She stepped close to Lee and spoke softly so Sammi and Ms. Hackett wouldn't overhear.

"I need to step out. Can you keep an ear on this?"

Lee gave her two thumbs up and Katherine slipped out of the office, jacket in hand.

She was pulling her jacket over her shoulders just as Jake's Jeep pulled up to the curb. Katherine hurried to his vehicle before he could turn the engine off. "Get us to the courthouse."

Jake shifted back into drive as Katherine buckled her seatbelt. "What's up?" he asked.

"I need to get to Margaret ASAP. The police have found their motive."

7

Katherine found Margaret pacing the hallway outside Assistant State's Attorney Heath Griffith's office.

"You just caught me, hon," Margaret said. Her tailored brown suit was slightly wrinkled after a long day, and her usually bright smile looked forced. "Heath's running late, as usual."

Katherine looked at her watch. "Good. We need to talk before you walk in there."

Margaret's eyes narrowed. "What happened?"

"Beth Taylor happened." Katherine lowered her voice, leaning closer. "She claims she was having an affair with James."

"That's ridiculous," Margaret scoffed. "James was devoted to Misty."

"There's more." Katherine paused to let the weight of her words register. "She says she's pregnant with his child."

Margaret froze mid-step. "No. Absolutely not. She's lying."

"She threatened to go to the police with it if we push too hard on her testimony." Katherine ran a hand through her hair. "And I just got a text from my contact at BPD. Beth made good on that threat an hour after we left her apartment."

Margaret stared at the closed door of Griffith's office. "That explains this sudden meeting." She squared her shoulders. "Misty can't have children. They tried for years before giving up. It was devastating for her."

Katherine groaned. "And you didn't think to mention this before?"

"It wasn't relevant until now," Margaret replied defensively. "And it's deeply personal."

The door to Griffith's office swung open, revealing the ASA's angular face and prematurely gray hair. His smug expression told Katherine everything she needed to know.

"Ms. Mitchell," he said with a thin smile. "And Ms. Carson. What a surprise."

Katherine stepped back. "I'll wait out here."

Ten minutes later, Margaret left Griffith's office. Her face was flushed with anger. Katherine jumped up from the bench where she had been waiting and followed her friend as she stormed down the hallway.

"Second-degree murder with a recommendation of fifteen years." Margaret's voice was tight with controlled fury. "He actually thinks that's generous."

"Based on the affair and the new motive?" Katherine asked, keeping her voice low.

"He says it's a 'crime of passion' now." Margaret stopped short to face Katherine, waving her arms as she spoke. "Claims he'd be doing Misty a favor by not pursuing first-degree. Says the jury will eat up the betrayal angle, especially with the pregnancy."

Katherine studied her friend's face. "You didn't accept."

"Of course not," Margaret snapped, then immediately softened. "I'm sorry, Kat. It's just … He was practically gloating about having this new ammunition. As if my friend's pain is just another notch in his conviction belt."

Katherine pressed the button for the elevator. "Did he ask you out to dinner again?" she asked, trying to lighten the mood.

Margaret rolled her eyes, some of her usual humor returning. "Right after offering my friend fifteen years. The man has terrible timing."

"Heath Griffith has had a crush on you since you passed the bar." Katherine laughed. "That's what, twelve years now?"

"Fourteen," Margaret corrected with a small smile. "And it's harmless. He asks, I decline, we move on. Say what you will about the man, he never lets it affect his work."

"Too bad," Katherine said dryly. "We could use the advantage."

Margaret's smile faded as they stepped onto the elevator. "If anything, he's harder on my clients to prove he's not playing favorites. Always has been."

"We need to talk to Misty," Katherine said, shifting back to the case. "Get her side of this."

"Absolutely not. Not until we verify whether this affair was real."

"She's our client, Mags," Katherine countered. "If she's been keeping this from us—"

"And what if she doesn't know?" Margaret challenged, an edge in her voice. "What then, Kat? I tell my college friend that her husband was not only cheating on her but also got another woman pregnant? While she's sitting in a jail cell accused of his murder? With the state dangling a plea deal that assumes her guilt?"

Katherine stood her ground. "If she doesn't know, then she deserves to hear it from us, not from Griffith when he's pressuring her to take that deal."

Margaret's shoulders drooped. "You're right. But let's at least confirm the affair first."

"Fine," Katherine conceded. "Tell me about the Bovills."

They stepped out into the courthouse lobby. Margaret sank onto a bench, suddenly looking exhausted.

"The three of them were inseparable in high school," she began. "Anna dated James before he left for college. Kyle was always the third wheel, competing with James for everything: grades, sports, even Anna's attention. Eventually, Kyle and Anna got together after James left. Kyle still competes with James. Whose car is faster, whose business was bigger. But they still seemed to maintain a genuine friendship."

"And years later, James hires his high school girlfriend as his executive assistant?" Katherine made a face. "That's either remarkably forgiving or remarkably stupid."

"When James moved back to Baltimore with Misty, he reconnected with his old friends." Margaret stood and pulled on her overcoat. "Misty always felt like an outsider with them. She told me once that whenever she had late nights at the museum, James would have dinner with Kyle and Anna."

"Anna was jealous of Misty?"

"Intensely," Margaret confirmed. "She's uncomfortably devoted to James."

"Romantically?"

"I don't think so. She seems to be committed to Kyle. But there's definitely an odd dynamic between them that I've never understood."

Katherine tightened her scarf as they stepped outside. "The pieces aren't fitting, Mags. The gun at the museum belonged to Misty, but she claims it should have been in their safe at home. James was teaching someone he called his assistant to shoot at the range. But Anna denies it was her. Beth claims to be having an affair with the victim, but withholds that from the police until it's convenient."

Margaret nodded. "Everyone in this case is hiding something."

"Including Misty," Katherine stated flatly.

"She's innocent, Kat." Margaret's voice hardened with conviction. "And I won't let her plead guilty to a crime she didn't commit, no matter what kind of 'generous' deal Heath is offering."

"I hope you're right." Katherine shrugged. "But until we uncover what everyone's hiding, we can't be sure of anything."

The courthouse parking lot had emptied as the afternoon stretched into early evening. Jake sat in the driver's seat of his Jeep, engine running to keep the heat circulating against the January chill. Light, lazy snowflakes caught the amber glow of streetlights just beginning to flicker on. Plumes of steam rose from the grate at the corner, evidence of the city's heating system working overtime.

Jake left a voice message for the Vanderlins' insurance broker to call him back the next day. Katherine wanted to know what they'd reported stolen. She was still looking for a loophole in the case against Mrs. Vanderlin. She would never admit it, but Jake suspected that Kat felt pressure to get this client off the hook since she is a friend of Margaret's.

Katherine's first line of work made it difficult to impossible for her to develop real friendships outside the intelligence community. He knew how much she valued her friendship with the pretty civilian defense attorney.

There. He said it. She's pretty. Gorgeous, actually. In fact, Jake had to admit to himself that Margaret Mitchell was probably the most beautiful woman he had ever met.

He sighed. That kind of thinking wouldn't get him anywhere. For one thing, Katherine was like his little sister. And Margaret was her best friend. What if he tried making a move, and it didn't work out? Then what?

And then there's the age gap. Jake didn't actually know how old Margaret was. That's not the kind of question you ask. He knew that she and Katherine met when they were little girls and Katherine visited her grandparents in Baltimore. So he assumed they were around the same age. He was eight, almost nine years older than Katherine.

Voices on the courthouse steps made him look up. He shook his head. Just a couple staff members leaving for the day.

Get a grip, Mercer. Jake pulled out his phone to keep his mind occupied. They'd heard about a night security guard who'd been fired from the Walters recently. Jake called to ask where he was the night of the murder.

The man on the other end of the line sounded exhausted. "Just got in from three weeks visiting my brother in Costa Rica. Still getting over the jet lag. Misty? Sure, I knew her. Nice lady. Had nothing to do with me leaving. I called in sick three days in a row. My kid had the flu, and my wife was working double shifts at the hospital. When I came back, they wanted to write me up for violating the attendance policy. So I quit. Job didn't pay enough for the hassle."

Jake thanked him and ended the call just as Katherine emerged from the courthouse with Margaret. They walked toward him, and he rolled down the window.

Katherine looked in. "You hungry? I was thinking we could all go to dinner."

Jake was suddenly hot everywhere in spite of the frigid breeze. "Sure." *Smooth, Mercer, real smooth.*

Katherine turned to look at Margaret, whose alabaster skin was flushed.

"Thanks for the invite," Margaret said, "but I have to get going."

Jake felt a mix of relief and disappointment. "Maybe next time," he said.

Margaret's face grew redder as she pulled her scarf up around her face and hurried down the sidewalk to her own car.

Katherine slid into the passenger seat, bringing a rush of cold air with her. "The ASA is offering a plea deal. Mags won't take it."

"The ex-night guard seems like a dead end," Jake said, putting the Jeep in drive. "He was in Costa Rica when Vanderlin was killed. Has documentation and witnesses."

Katherine buckled her seatbelt. "Another theory down."

Jake turned onto Charles Street, the familiar rhythm of investigation settling over them both. Another lead eliminated. But that was progress too. Each dead end narrowed their focus, bringing them closer to the truth.

Even if they didn't know what that truth was yet.

8

The wrought-iron gates of the Baltimore Highlands estate parted with a mechanical whir. Jake steered his Jeep up the curved driveway, gravel crunching beneath the tires. The Georgian-style mansion loomed ahead, lit by harsh floodlights against the winter darkness.

"Raymond Harwick." Katherine checked her notes. "Chair of the board at the Walters for nearly a decade. Independently wealthy, made his fortune in commercial real estate develop-ment."

Jake nodded, his eyes scanning the property as he parked. "Nothing like a command performance," he grumbled, thinking of the half-finished dinner they had left behind.

Katherine looked at her watch. "We're lucky he agreed to see us at all. His assistant said they're leaving for DC in a couple hours."

The massive front door opened before they could ring the bell. A tall, silver-haired man in a tailored charcoal suit extended his hand.

"Detectives, I presume?" The man's voice carried the polished cadence of old money. "Raymond Harwick. Please come in. My wife has me on a strict schedule this evening."

Katherine and Jake showed their identification and stepped into the marble-floored foyer.

Harwick led them through an entrance hall adorned with museum-quality paintings. "I've allocated twenty minutes for this conversation. I understand you're investigating James Vanderlin's murder?" He checked his Rolex watch. "Nasty business. The museum community is still in shock."

A woman's voice called out from somewhere upstairs. "Ray! Have you seen my sapphire earrings? The ones the Goldmans gave us last Christmas?"

"Check your jewelry case, Elaine," Harwick called back, then gestured toward a study off the main hall. "Please, let's talk in here. My wife is thrilled about attending the inauguration. First African-American president ... historic moment and all that."

The study was masculine and traditional, filled with leather-bound books, a massive mahogany desk, and the unmistakable scent of expensive cigars. Harwick closed the door, muffling the sounds of his wife's preparations.

"I'm afraid I have limited information about James's personal life," Harwick admitted, settling into a leather chair and motioning for them to sit on the sofa opposite. "Our relationship was primarily professional."

Katherine leaned forward. "We understand James served on the board with you at the Walters."

"Yes, we invited him to join us about ten years ago. Brilliant mind for Renaissance art. His expertise was invaluable." Harwick's expression was neutral. "A tragic loss for the museum world. And for Misty, of course."

"Did James ever mention any problems at the museum? Disagreements with staff or other board members?" Katherine asked.

Harwick's fingers drummed twice on the arm of his chair before he caught himself and stopped. "Nothing out of the ordinary. Museums always have their share of personality conflicts and budget disputes."

Jake caught a slight tightening around Harwick's mouth. "I spoke with Derrick Freeman yesterday. He mentioned something about a disputed acquisition."

The room went silent except for the ticking of an antique grandfather clock. Outside the study door, footsteps hurried past, followed by the sound of a suitcase being dragged across hardwood floors.

"Ah, yes." Harwick sighed. "The Botticelli sketch. That was… contentious."

"How so?" Katherine prompted.

"The museum acquired it last spring from a private collector in Florence. James was initially enthusiastic. He had a particular fondness for Botticelli. But about two months later, he came to me with concerns about its authenticity." Harwick stood and walked to a sidebar where he poured himself a small glass of water. He didn't offer any to his visitors.

"What happened then?" Jake asked.

"We did what any reputable institution would do. We assembled a team of experts to re-examine the piece." Harwick sipped his water. "The department was divided. Misty, as head curator, stood by the acquisition. But James and a few others insisted further testing was warranted."

"And the outcome?" Katherine pressed.

"We're still awaiting final results from a specialized lab in Switzerland." Harwick's tone was clipped. "It became rather heated at times. James was passionate about artistic integrity."

The door burst open, and a slender woman in her early sixties swept in, wearing an elegant wool suit. Her hair was perfectly coiffed, her makeup impeccable.

"Ray, the car service just called. They'll be here in an hour and—" She stopped, noticing Katherine and Jake. "Oh! I didn't realize you had company."

"These are private investigators, dear. Regarding James Vanderlin's murder." Harwick's tone softened slightly. "This is my wife, Elaine."

Elaine's hand flew to her throat. "Oh! How dreadful. Poor James. And poor Misty—she must be devastated."

Jake noticed the quick glance Harwick shot his wife.

"Yes, Mrs. Vanderlin is taking it hard," Katherine said.

"Well, of course she is," Elaine continued, seemingly oblivious to her husband's discomfort. "Though I imagine Beth is taking it just as hard. She's Misty's assistant curator, you know."

"Beth Taylor," Harwick supplied, his jaw tightening. "Yes, she was the one who first brought up questions about the sketch's authenticity. They worked closely on the research."

"Very closely, from what I heard," Elaine added, her eyebrows lifting. "She and James, I mean. Perhaps too closely."

"Elaine," Harwick said sharply. "I'm sure the detectives aren't interested in staff emotions."

Katherine exchanged a quick glance with Jake. "Actually, Mrs. Harwick, that might be relevant. What exactly did you hear about Mr. Vanderlin and Ms. Taylor?"

Elaine perched on the arm of her husband's chair. "Well, I don't like to gossip, but—"

"Then don't," Harwick interjected.

"Raymond." Elaine patted his shoulder. "A man is dead. If I know something that might help ..." She turned back to Katherine. "It was at the museum's winter gala. I went to the ladies' room and overheard Beth on her phone in one of the stalls. She was clearly upset, saying something like, 'You can't keep this from her forever, James. It isn't fair to any of us'."

"And this was when?" Katherine asked.

"December. Just before Christmas."

Jake shifted to face the husband. "Mr. Harwick, did you know about this ... relationship?"

Harwick's shoulders stiffened. "I suspected. James had become distracted during board meetings. Always checking his phone. And there were times I'd come to the museum after hours for paperwork, and they'd both still be there, working late." He paused. "I never confronted him directly. It wasn't my place to interfere in his personal life."

"But it affected his professional judgment?" Katherine pressed.

"I didn't say that," Harwick responded cautiously.

"But he seemed to take her opinion a bit too seriously ... considering that his wife has a doctorate in art history and Beth has yet to complete her Master's." Elaine spoke in a stage whisper, ignoring her husband's stern look. "No one had any reason to question the work's authenticity until she brought it up."

The grandfather clock chimed the half-hour. Harwick stood. "I'm afraid we need to finish packing. The President-elect's staff arranged special seating for arts patrons at tomorrow's ceremony."

"Just one more question," Katherine said, rising as well. "Did James mention any specific concerns about the authentication process? Perhaps someone who might have been threatened by his investigation?"

Harwick hesitated, then shook his head. "Not to me. But ..." He glanced at his wife, who nodded. "You might want to speak with Dr. Leonid Volkov. He's our conservation scientist. He and James had several closed-door meetings in the weeks before James was killed."

"And where can we find Dr. Volkov?" Jake asked.

"At the museum's conservation lab," Elaine supplied. "Basement level, east wing."

"So," Jake said as they walked out, "other board members knew something was going on between James and Beth." There was a lot more to Beth Taylor than it would seem on the surface.

Katherine pressed her lips together. "We need to talk to Dr. Volkov, find out what concerns with the Botticelli sketch Beth presented, and whether they had any validity. Or if she manipulated James into the investigation to make Misty look bad."

9

Sammi clutched her coffee thermos with both hands, grateful for its warmth as she hurried to the Carson Investigations office. Her breath fogged in front of her as she fumbled with the keys.

The office was silent and dark. Sammi flicked on the lights and cranked up the ancient radiator, listening to it tick and groan as it sluggishly came to life. 6:52 AM. She'd beaten everyone by at least an hour. Perfect.

The snow outside continued to fall in lazy spirals, coating the Baltimore streets in a thin, white blanket. She shrugged off her puffy coat and unwound the colorful scarf from around her neck, hanging them on a hook near the door.

Sammi booted up one of the office computers and took a fortifying sip of her cafe con leche.

"Okay, Judith and Holofernes," she said to the empty office. Her fingers flew across the keyboard. "Let's see what you're all about."

Her search returned dozens of images—all variations of the same gruesome scene. A beautiful woman holding a sword in one hand and the severed head of a man in the other. In some versions, an elderly servant woman stood nearby, her face a mask of grim determination.

"Yikes," Sammi whispered, leaning closer to the screen. "Talk about your revenge fantasies."

Half an hour later, Sammi had learned everything she could about the history of the subject and the specific painting in the Waters Museum. She organized her notes to share with the team later. Other than the fact that Misty Vanderlin spearheaded the acquisition of the painting, she couldn't find a connection to the Vanderlins. They didn't have any Jewish heritage or a particular connection to the artist or the seller of the painting.

Sammi took a break to wash her thermos and brew a fresh pot of coffee. Then she turned her attention to their newest case. She started with a basic background check on Christopher Euler, then moved on to social media. LinkedIn showed him working at Mason & Blackwell Accounting for the past five years. Nothing unusual there. His Facebook profile was barely used. The last update was eight months ago with a vacation photo of him and Cynthia in Ocean City. No other social media.

She dug deeper, using the username CEuler78 which Cynthia had shared with her last night. A hit on a forum for classic car enthusiasts. Another on an online fantasy football league. Nothing suspicious.

Her phone buzzed with a text from Lee. "Morning, chica. When you get in, run background on Gavin Tucker, DOB 6/14/85. Need basics ASAP"

She smiled at the screen, imagining Lee in his element, charming information out of the museum staff with that slow Georgia drawl.

She texted back immediately. "Already here! On it."

Sammi turned back to her computer. Gavin Tucker. She hadn't heard that name before. Maybe a new client? Or someone new connected to the Vanderlin murder?

Whoever he was, Gavin was more interesting than Mr. Euler. He was a year younger than Sammi. A Maryland University graduate who had worked in IT help desk support since high school. Currently employed by SecureTech Solutions, a computer hardware company specializing in custom technology system setups.

"Bingo," Sammi whispered.

"Appreciate you meeting me so early," Lee said, settling into a chair and unwrapping his scarf.

"Not a problem, Mr. Stewart." Security Chief Frank Naylor was sitting at his desk. His office walls were lined with security monitors showing empty galleries. "If there's anything I can do to help clear Misty's name, I'm all in. This whole situation doesn't add up."

Lee nodded, studying the man's face. "Tell me about Misty Vanderlin. Your professional assessment."

"Twelve years as our curator. Came here from New York. Albany, I think. They relocated specifically for this position." His expression softened with respect. "She transformed our collections. Patient. Meticulous."

Lee jotted notes in a small leather-bound notebook. "And James supported the move? Twelve years is a considerable commitment."

"Absolutely. He was her champion from day one. Joined our board about ten years back, threw himself into fundraising."

Naylor gestured toward a framed photo on the wall showing a ribbon-cutting ceremony. "That's them at the opening of the Renaissance Gallery. James always said her career was their shared mission."

"Makes the accusation all the more puzzling," Lee murmured, tapping his pen against the notebook. "The idea she'd murder him in her own exhibit."

"Exactly. And just a week before her crowning achievement." Naylor shook his head. "The Baroque exhibit was to be her legacy piece. James was beyond proud, even funded our new security upgrade as an opening gift."

Lee scratched his ear. "Interesting timing. When exactly was this upgrade installed?"

"Just completed last week. Was supposed to be a surprise enhancement for the opening."

"Mind if I take a look at the specifics?" Lee was a technical enthusiast and would have been interested in the new system even without the open murder investigation.

The security chief tapped at his keyboard. "I can print you the full report. Installation dates, camera locations, the works."

"Sounds great." Lee smiled. "Who handled the installation?"

"Company called SecureTech Solutions. Young technician named Gavin Tucker did most of the work." He pulled up another file and hit print. "Nice enough guy, knew his stuff."

"How'd they get the contract? Museum must have procurement procedures."

Naylor shrugged, spreading his hands. "James had connections with one of the owners. Pulled some strings to fast-track it."

"Y'all meet with this Tucker fella much during installation?"

"Spoke on the phone several times. Met him briefly to go over specs." Naylor collected papers from the printer and slid them across the desk. "Our paths didn't cross during the actual install. We were supposed to do final inspection on Thursday before the opening gala on Friday night."

Lee raised an eyebrow. "That's quite a gap between install and inspection, isn't it?"

"Tucker's on vacation. Washington DC this week." Naylor shrugged. "Something about the inauguration events."

"So you've been running a brand-new security system without inspection for," Lee glanced at the installation dates, "going on seven days now?"

Frank Naylor rubbed the back of his neck. "Look, I'll be straight with you. The technical side isn't my strong suit. Twenty years military police, I understand protocol and personnel. But these digital systems? I trusted the company James selected."

Lee nodded slowly, his mind racing. "Might I trouble you for the security logs? Both systems—the old one for a couple days prior and everything from the new one."

"Everything?" Frank Naylor asked, surprised. "That's a lot of data. What exactly are you looking for in all that footage?" he asked with a skeptical laugh.

"In my experience, when technology's involved, the devil's always hiding in the data."

His fingers drummed lightly on the arm of the chair as Naylor began the process of extracting the security logs. The truth was, Lee didn't know what he was looking for. A pattern, an anomaly ... a smoking gun. That was what drew him to data analysis in the first place. The not knowing. And then finding something everyone else missed.

Lee studied the wall of monitors, his trained eye noting the camera angles, blind spots, and the darkened Baroque gallery where James Vanderlin had spent his final moments.

"Y'know," Lee said quietly, "I find it mighty coincidental that a man buys a new security system, then turns up dead in the very space it was meant to protect."

Naylor stopped typing, looking up sharply. "You think the security upgrade is connected to the murder?"

"I don't believe in coincidences, Chief." Lee accepted the flash drive Naylor handed him. "Not when the stakes are this high and the timing is this precise." He pocketed the drive and stood to leave. "One more thing, this Gavin Tucker. Got a contact number? Might want to interrupt his little vacation in DC."

10

The headquarters of Meridian Tech was located in Baltimore's historic district. Jake admired the exposed brick walls and original timber beams in the reception area. The converted textile mill reminded him of an abandoned factory in Kosovo that his Ranger unit had repurposed as a forward operating base. Same solid bones, different purpose.

He showed his ID to the receptionist, a smiling middle-aged woman with sensible glasses. "I'm Jake Mercer, a private detective. I have an appointment with Mr. Lacroix."

"Yes, of course." Her smile faded. "Regarding Mr. Vanderlin? Such a terrible thing. He was always so kind when he came through."

"You knew him well?"

"Five years at this desk," she said, picking up the phone. "Mr. Vanderlin remembered my granddaughter's name every time he asked about her. Not many executives like that." After making sure Mr. Lacroix was in, she escorted Jake to the CEO's office at the back of the old building.

Owen Lacroix's office was comfortable but not extravagant, with large windows overlooking the harbor. Family photos lined one shelf, and a well-worn baseball sat in a display case.

"Mr. Mercer," Lacroix greeted him with a brief handshake and a tight smile. "Please, sit down." He gestured to the chair. "Can I offer you coffee? I was just about to ..." He turned toward the carafe.

"Thank you," Jake said, studying him. Lacroix wore a conventional business suit with a Baltimore Orioles tie pin that he kept adjusting as if it were crooked. "Black, if that's all right."

The CEO was older than Jake had expected, probably mid-fifties, with flecks of gray in his close-cropped beard. Lacroix's fingers drummed against his leg as he poured from a carafe on a side table. He nearly overfilled the cup, pulling back just in time.

"Terrible business, this," Lacroix said, handing Jake the coffee before checking his watch. "James was ..." He paused and looked out the window. "Well, he was more than, uh, more than a colleague, obviously." He loosened his tie, then immediately tightened it again.

Jake took a sip, buying time to assess Lacroix's reaction. Eight years as a private detective had taught him that guilt and grief often look remarkably similar.

"You worked together for how long?"

"Twelve years since—or no, let me think—yes, twelve years since we founded Meridian Tech," Lacroix replied, settling behind his desk. "But we've known each other much longer. Columbia University days." He reached for a folder on his desk and closed it, sliding it into a drawer.

"You, James, and Misty all attended Columbia?" Jake confirmed.

"That's right. James and I were in business school together. Second career for me. Misty was studying art history, beautiful campus there in New York, really extraordinary architecture ..." He trailed off, seemed to realize he was rambling, and dabbed at his forehead with a handkerchief he pulled from his pocket. "We all moved back to Baltimore after graduation. Misty got the job at the Walters. James and Misty got married, and a year later, he and I launched Meridian."

"Partners from the beginning?" Jake took a large swallow of the hot coffee.

"James was our visionary and relationship builder. I handled operations and technical implementation." A fond smile crossed his face before fading into something more troubled. "He could read a room better than anyone I've ever known. Clients trusted him instinctively." Lacroix suddenly stood and walked to the thermostat. "Is it warm in here to you?"

"I'm comfortable. And your personal relationship?"

"Friends. Good friends, very good." He adjusted his tie pin as he walked back to the desk. "Look, Mr. Mercer, I want to help Misty. This whole situation is absurd. She couldn't have killed James, not Misty, never." Lacroix's fingers found a pen on his desk, clicking it several times before catching himself and setting it down.

Jake nodded, letting the statement stand. "Let's talk about James's business dealings. Any conflicts with clients or competitors in recent months? Someone who might have had a grievance?"

Lacroix's gaze focused on the baseball in its display case rather than on Jake. "James had a talent for smoothing over difficult situations, but ..." He rearranged a stack of business cards. "There was that situation with the Westlake account.

James discovered ..." He cleared his throat. "Or rather, James noticed some, ah, irregularities in their financial reporting, quietly dropped them as clients. No public accusation, but they knew he knew. But that was two years ago. Ancient history, really." His eyes flicked to his watch again.

"Anyone else who might have had reason to want James out of the picture?" Jake asked.

Lacroix began to respond, stopped, took a sip of water, then started again, seeming to weigh each word. "There was tension with Carrington Systems. We outbid them on the NetSphere acquisition last quarter. James's strategy, his contacts. Their CEO, Wilbur Carrington, made some thinly veiled threats at an industry event." His eyes darted away. "But murder over business? That seems extreme, even in our competitive industry, doesn't it? Though I suppose stranger things have happened in corporate America. The pressure these days is just extraordinary, and executives like Wilbur, well, they're not always the most stable." He stopped abruptly.

"People have killed for less," Jake said. "What can you tell me about James's role here these last few months? Any changes in behavior? New tensions?"

Lacroix adjusted his coffee cup. "James was ... James. Brilliant with clients, instinctive with market—" His phone buzzed, and he glanced at it before turning it face down. "Sorry about that. Instinctive with market trends." He hesitated, pulling at his collar. "But something was off. Since July, maybe." He stood suddenly, walking to the window before turning back. "Or June. Possibly June."

"Off how?"

"Distracted. Missing meetings he would never have missed before. Taking calls in the stairwell rather than his office."

Lacroix crossed his arms, then put his hands in his pockets. "I asked him about it once. He laughed it off, said he was working on something that would 'change everything.' His words, not mine." He crossed his arms again. "I didn't pry further, of course."

"Did he ever tell you more about this project that would change everything?"

"No." Lacroix walked back to his desk. "James could be secretive when he wanted to be." He sat down again. "I assumed it was another tech acquisition. He was always researching something. Always looking at the next opportunity. Very forward-thinking, James." He picked up the pen again, flicking the clip with his thumbnail.

"What about Anna Bovill? How would you characterize her relationship with James?"

The pen slipped from Lacroix's hand, clattering to the desk. He fumbled to pick it up, nearly knocking over his coffee in the process. "Anna is excellent at her job. Very professional. Dedicated. Been with us from the beginning."

"That's not what I asked."

Lacroix set the pen down carefully, aligning it precisely parallel to the edge of the desk. "It's complicated." His knee began bouncing under the desk. "Anna was our first hire, actually. She's been with us, with him, really, ever since."

"Moving up the ranks?"

"Well, sort of ... She's officially his executive assistant now, but her role evolved beyond that years ago," Lacroix said, his words coming faster now. "She's practically a shadow executive, handling sensitive matters, sitting in on key meetings. James trusts—" He visibly winced. "Trusted her completely," he corrected himself. "They worked well together. Very professional. Nothing inappropriate. James was always professional." The repetition hung awkwardly in the air.

"Just worked?" Jake pressed.

"I never saw anything inappropriate, if that's what you're asking." Lacroix's words tumbled out too quickly as he rearranged the business cards, pens, and files on his desk. "But Anna was ... devoted. Perhaps overly so. Not that I'm suggesting anything, understand? Just an observation."

"Meaning?"

Lacroix sighed, rubbing his temple, then the back of his neck. "James relied on her completely. She managed everything for him. His schedule, his correspondence, his travel arrangements. Even personal matters sometimes."

"Like what?"

"Birthday gifts for Misty. Dinner reservations. Sometimes even helping with investment research for his personal portfolio." Lacroix picked up his coffee cup for the first time since he'd filled it. "Nothing unusual for an executive assistant, but there was an intensity to it. Not that there's anything wrong with being dedicated to your job, of course. I value loyalty tremendously in our organization."

Jake nodded. "Any conflicts between James and Anna recently?"

A long pause followed. Lacroix stared at his coffee, turning the cup slowly in his hands. "There was an incident. One day I came in early and found Anna at James's computer. She claimed she was updating his calendar, but when I glanced at the screen, it looked like financial records. Not that I was snooping, you understand. Just happened to notice."

"Did you mention this to James?"

"I did. He said he'd asked her to pull some data for him." Lacroix didn't sound convinced, his foot now tapping rapidly under the desk.

"But you didn't believe him?"

"James was a terrible liar," Lacroix said with unexpected fondness. "Always had been. Something was bothering him, but he wouldn't share it. Not with me, anyway." He set the coffee cup down without drinking. "Look, Mr. Mercer, I'm not suggesting Anna did anything wrong. She was—is—devoted to this company. Completely loyal."

"Just like she was devoted to James."

Lacroix didn't answer directly. "The last few weeks, something changed between them. The easy rapport was gone. James started locking his office door. Taking calls outside." He stared at the windows. "Anna seemed upset. Angry."

"Like someone whose trust had been betrayed?"

"Or like someone who felt she was losing her place," Lacroix countered too quickly. His hand went to his tie pin again.

"Mr. Lacroix," Jake said quietly, "I get the impression there's something you're not telling me."

The CEO stared at him for a long moment. Jake let the silence expand between them, a technique he'd perfected during hundreds of security clearance interviews for the NSA. The weight of unspoken words always pressed hardest on those with something to hide.

Lacroix suddenly stood and adjusted the window blinds. When he returned to his desk, he spoke in a low voice. "James came to me about two months ago." His eyes were fixed on the baseball in its case. "Asked me how we'd handle a potential scandal involving the firm. Hypothetically, he emphasized." Lacroix's knuckles whitened around his coffee mug as he picked it up and moved it to another spot on the desk. "He wouldn't give details, just wanted to know about our crisis management protocols."

Jake remained silent, letting him continue.

"Very hypothetical, he said. Just a thought exercise, really." Lacroix babbled as his discomfort increased. The man was wound tighter than a tripwire, and just as close to snapping.

"Did he give any indication of what this hypothetical scandal might be?" Jake asked.

"I asked him, but all he would say was that he was looking into something that might have 'significant implications.' His words, not mine." Lacroix hesitated. He checked his phone again, this time keeping it in his hand. "I should mention that a client call is coming up very soon."

Jake nodded. "One last question. With James gone, what happens to his share of the company?"

Lacroix's professional demeanor reasserted itself, though he continued to fidget with his phone. "Our partnership agreement is standard. His shares would go to his estate. Misty, presumably. With the remaining partner, me, having first option to purchase at fair market value. All very straightforward, nothing unusual."

"And if Misty is convicted?" Jake asked bluntly.

A flash of genuine distress crossed Lacroix's face. "That's not going to happen. It can't." He stood abruptly, nearly knocking over his chair. "I'm sorry, Mr. Mercer, but I have a client call right now." He glanced at his watch. "Right now, actually. I'm already late."

Jake rose unhurriedly. "Thank you for your time." He slid a business card across the desk. "If you think of anything else."

Lacroix locked eyes with Jake. "Find who did this, Mr. Mercer. James deserves justice. And Misty ..." His voice crackled. "Misty doesn't deserve any of this. None of us do."

He was already holding his phone as Jake left, his hand shaking as he punched in a number.

11

Katherine tapped her notebook on the edge of Rhonda Eden's desk. "So you think Misty knew about the affair?" Katherine asked. "Enough to convince Margaret to have that conversation with our client?"

The police detective's laugh came out like a short bark. "Husbands and wives killing each other over affairs? That's Tuesday in Baltimore, hon." She shuffled through some cluttered papers. "And yeah, we've confirmed Misty knew. Made quite the scene at a Halloween party when someone let it slip."

"Who told her?"

"Still tracking that down. We've been canvassing her friends, trying to nail down the timeline." Rhonda's eyes met Katherine's. "Looking for motive."

Katherine sighed. "Any evidence of premeditation?"

Rhonda leaned back in her chair. "I know the ASA offered you a plea deal." She tapped her coffee mug, a chipped thing with the Baltimore PD shield. "So far, we haven't found anything concrete pointing to premeditation, but it's only a matter of time. Had to be planned." She paused. "Margaret has no intention of taking any deal, does she?"

"She seems unusually invested," Katherine conceded.

"That's putting it mildly."

Katherine shifted the subject. "We're looking into two other women as suspects with motives. Beth Taylor and Anna Bovill."

Rhonda shook her head, smirking. "And what motives would those be?"

"Misty's motive and Beth's are identical. Both in relationships with James, both jealous of the other." Katherine kept her voice even. "And it's possible Anna was involved with him too. They were together in high school."

"That's pretty thin," Rhonda argued.

Katherine shrugged. "Sometimes thin is all you've got until it thickens." She paused. "Can I see the file on the Vanderlins' home break-in from last year?"

Rhonda laughed, reaching for her phone. "File clerk's gonna love me today." She punched in the extension number with precision. As she waited for an answer, she turned back to Katherine. "One thing's for sure, Kat. Whoever shot Vanderlin really knew how to handle a gun." She made a pistol with her finger and thumb. "One bullet. Perfect shot. No powder burns."

While Rhonda rose to collect the file, Katherine's mind drifted back to the day Daniel had decided to teach her to shoot.

"We'll start with basics," Daniel said. "Stance, grip, sight alignment ..."

"Look who decided to grace us with her presence!" Jake Mercer's voice boomed across the lobby. He walked up with an easy grin. "Haven't seen you around the range lately, Kat."

Katherine shrugged. "Been busy."

"Agent Carson, good to see you," Jake said as he shook Daniel's hand.

"We're here for a shooting lesson," Daniel explained.

Jake's eyes went wide. "Daniel's going to teach you to shoot, huh?"

"That's the plan," Daniel replied.

"This, I've gotta see." Jake's eyes darted between them. He caught Katherine's eye and winked, clearly amused.

Daniel led them to lane seven, methodically unpacking his range bag. "We'll start with the Glock 17. Standard issue, manageable recoil."

"Whatever you think is best." Katherine replied demurely as she donned ear protection.

Jake leaned against the wall behind them with his arms crossed. "I'll just watch from back here."

Daniel demonstrated the proper grip. "Now, align the front sight with the rear notch. Keep both eyes open, focus on the front sight, not the target."

Katherine nodded solemnly as she accepted the weapon.

"Let's see what we're working with," Daniel said. "Just try to hit the paper. Don't worry about grouping yet."

Katherine took position, her stance casual. She raised the pistol, took a long, slow breath, and fired six rounds in rapid succession.

Daniel's jaw went slack as he pressed the button to retrieve the target. Six holes formed a tight cluster directly over the silhouette's center mass, none more than half an inch from the others.

"That was..." He cleared his throat. "Beginner's luck. Let's try something more challenging."

Jake chuckled, unable to contain himself any longer. "Come on, Carson, let's see what she can really do. Set up the Agency qual course."

Daniel cocked an eyebrow. "That's advanced operator level."

Jake clapped him on the shoulder. "Trust me."

Katherine was already loading fresh magazines. Daniel programmed the course, and she took her position.

At the signal, she moved through the course with ease, her body and weapon functioning as a single unit. She maintained a proper fighting stance, elbows slightly bent to absorb recoil, and utilized tactical breathing to control her heart rate between firing positions. She transitioned smoothly from primary to secondary weapon during a simulated malfunction. She hit every threat target with center mass double-taps followed by a failure drill head shot when necessary, avoided every non-threat target through proper target discrimination, and maintained muzzle discipline during movement phases.

Katherine completed the course in a time that would have qualified her for elite tactical teams.

Daniel watched, transfixed, as she holstered her weapon.

"My father gave me my first firearm when I was seven," she said, echoing their earlier conversation. "Two years after the knife."

Jake burst into laughter at Daniel's expression. "You should see your face, man! Did you really think the daughter of Edwin and Katerina Goillot couldn't shoot?"

Daniel's face flushed. "You could have mentioned something."

"You never asked if I could shoot," Katherine replied. "You assumed I couldn't. There's a difference."

"She outscored me three years running at the Inter-Agency championships," Jake added helpfully. "And I was East Coast combat shooting champion before joining the NSA."

Daniel ran a hand through his hair, embarrassment and admiration battling across his features. "Why let me make a fool of myself?"

Katherine stepped closer, close enough to let him smell her sweat beneath the gunpowder. "Because you wanted to teach me something. And I wanted to see what kind of teacher you'd be."

"And?" Daniel asked, swallowing hard.

Jake cleared his throat loudly. "And that's my cue to remind you both that Katie is basically my sister, Carson." His tone was light, but his eyes conveyed a clear warning. "Which means I'm contractually obligated to make your life miserable if necessary."

Katherine rolled her eyes. "I can handle myself, Jake."

"Oh, I know," Jake replied, his gaze still locked with Daniel's. "Just making sure everyone else knows too."

Daniel nodded, his eyes sparkling with a newfound respect.

"So," Katherine said, breaking the tension as she checked her watch. "Since we've established I don't need shooting lessons, how about lunch? I'm famished."

"Earth to Katherine." Rhonda's voice snapped her back. The detective dropped a manila folder on the desk between them. "File's here. You okay? Looked like you were a million miles away."

Katherine flipped open the folder and scanned the break-in report.

Rhonda settled back into her chair. "Nothing much taken. Some jewelry, electronics, standard stuff." She tapped her coffee mug. "We figured it for a random hit."

Katherine pursed her lips as she turned a page. "A window was broken, but the alarm wasn't tripped."

"Someone who knew the code," Rhonda acknowledged with a slight nod. "Or someone left the alarm off. We looked at the housekeeper, the landscaper. Nothing stuck. And before you ask, the safe wasn't touched. Her gun wasn't stolen."

"Touché." Katherine closed the folder. "Misty's gun ... the murder weapon. When was the last time it was fired before the museum?"

Rhonda smiled. "According to range records, about nine months ago. Vanderlin had a membership at Charm City Gun Club."

"I heard that Misty wasn't a very good shot." Katherine watched Rhonda's reaction.

"A lot can change in nine months," Rhonda said, narrowing her eyes. "Either Misty's been secretly practicing somewhere else, or—"

"Or someone who knew how to shoot used her gun," Katherine finished.

Rhonda nodded slowly. "But that still doesn't explain how Misty was there, or why her prints were on the weapon."

"People touch their own guns, Rhonda. And we know why she was at the museum."

"Right where her husband got shot," Rhonda countered. "With her gun."

"Margaret Mitchell doesn't bet on long shots." Katherine stood, adjusting the strap of her bag. "Thanks for the info."

Rhonda stood as well. "Don't make me regret it." She paused. "And Kat? Whatever you find, I get first look."

"This is Margaret's case," Katherine reminded her. "I just work for her."

"Bullshit." Rhonda chuckled. "This is your case the moment you decided Misty might be innocent." She held Katherine's gaze. "What changed your mind?"

Katherine considered the detective for a moment. "The shot."

"What about it?"

"One bullet, perfect placement." Katherine tapped her forehead with her index finger. "That's not luck, that's not passion."

"It's cold."

"Exactly." Katherine nodded. "Too cold for what they're selling. And whoever did it wanted us to think it was Misty."

"But we've got her at the scene."

"Yes," Katherine agreed. "But what if she was set up before she ever walked into that gallery?"

Rhonda crossed her arms. "That's a hell of a theory to prove."

"I've worked with less." Katherine winked. "I'll be in touch."

$$12$$

Lee Stewart followed the security chief through the museum's marble-floored hall near the Charles Street Entrance, the steady click of their shoes echoing off the vaulted ceiling.

"Mrs. Abernathy has been volunteering at the check-in desk for—how long is it now, Eleanor?" The security chief gestured toward an elegant silver-haired woman seated behind a polished mahogany desk.

"Seventeen years next month, Frank," she said with a smile that crinkled the corners of her eyes. Her hands were neatly folded atop a visitor logbook, fingers adorned with vintage rings that caught the light.

"She's seen everything and everyone who's come through those doors," Frank continued. "If your man Gavin was here regularly, Eleanor would have noticed."

Lee's posture softened as he approached, the tension in his shoulders giving way to the easy charm he reserved for interviews. "Mrs. Abernathy, I reckon you're the most valuable security system this museum's got."

Eleanor Abernathy's expression brightened. "And you are?"

"Lee Stewart, ma'am. I'm investigating a matter that might involve a technician who worked here. Mind if I ask you a few questions?"

"Not at all, young man." She gestured to a chair beside her desk. "Frank, I'll be fine here. You go on back to your rounds."

The security chief nodded and retreated, leaving Lee alone with the volunteer.

"I understand you're here most days," Lee began. "Would've been hard to miss a fella coming in regularly to work on security systems."

"Oh, the chubby one," Eleanor said immediately, leaning forward with a conspiratorial gleam in her brown eyes. "Said his name was Gavin. Always carrying those toolboxes and computer things. Crawling around in our ceilings and walls all last week." She lowered her voice. "Between us, I thought he looked like he spent more time with video games than actual exercise. Pale as a ghost."

Lee chuckled. "Sounds like our guy. Did he interact much with the staff here?"

"Not really. I take it that everything was planned out ahead of time." She waved her hand in a circle, indicating the new security system. "He asked about Curator Vanderlin—that's Misty—once or twice when she was out. He may have spoken to Beth Taylor, the assistant curator." Eleanor's mouth formed a tight line. "Those two, now there's a situation."

"How do you mean?" Lee asked.

"Beth imagines they're rivals. Always trying to outshine Misty, making little comments. But Misty's real class—degree from the New York Institute of Fine Arts, worked hard to be where she is. Married for love, not money." Eleanor adjusted one of her rings. "Beth's all designer labels with the tags still showing, if you catch my meaning. Fake. You can tell."

"And Misty's been here what, ten years?"

"Twelve years this spring," Eleanor said with authority. "Built this place into what it is today. Beth's only been here two years, maybe three. Still thinks she knows everything." She sniffed disapprovingly.

"And this new security system…?"

"Oh yes, very exciting." Eleanor's eyes lit up with the pleasure of having valuable information. "A gift from Misty's husband. Top of the line, Frank said. That young man—Gavin—he was installing it everywhere. Said it would protect our collections better than anything on the market."

"Did Curator Vanderlin seem to know the details of the installation? Was she involved?"

"No, it was supposed to be a surprise for the opening. Her husband is on the board, so he arranged it with Frank and whoever else makes these decisions. This was his way of supporting her work."

Lee tilted his head slightly. "So Mrs. Vanderlin didn't know about the new security system?"

"Not that I know of." Eleanor paused, considering. "They asked us not to mention it to her. She's been distracted, what with the big gallery opening this week. Assuming it still opens." The wrinkles in her forehead grew deeper as she frowned.

"Back to Gavin. Did he ever meet with anyone else here? Have visitors?"

Eleanor shook her head. "Not that I saw. He'd just check in, get to work, and leave without much fuss. Polite enough, though he barely looked up from that phone of his." She made a dismissive gesture. "Young people and their screens. I don't understand the appeal of all this technology. In my day, we had actual conversations."

Lee suppressed a smile. "Technology has its place, ma'am, though I reckon there's no substitute for observant folks like yourself. Human intelligence is always the most valuable kind."

Eleanor preened at the compliment. "That's exactly what I always say. These computers can't notice things like a trained eye. For instance, Gavin always carried the same battered thermos. Coffee stains on his shirt cuffs. And he had this habit of whistling when he thought no one was listening—show tunes, I believe."

Lee raised an eyebrow. She was indeed observant. "You've been incredibly helpful, Mrs. Abernathy." He rose from his chair, producing a business card. "If you remember anything else about Gavin, or notice anything unusual around here, would you give me a call?"

"I certainly will, Mr. Stewart." She accepted the card with a pleased smile, slipping it into a small drawer.

As he walked away, Lee's mind was already processing the information, sorting relevant details from gossip, constructing a timeline of Gavin's activities. The rivalry between the curators was interesting, given Beth's relationship with James. And Misty's knowledge of the security installation ... that was worth exploring. If she didn't know where the new cameras were located, that could explain some of her actions from the night of the murder. Assuming the police theory was correct. On the other hand, if she was innocent, then Gavin's involvement in the setup was even more significant.

Lee flipped open his Nokia and dialed the number Frank Naylor had given him. Time to find out about this Gavin character. One way or another.

13

Lee spent the rest of the morning conducting interviews in the museum offices. The pristine white walls and hushed conversations created an atmosphere more like a library than a workplace. He visited each department, piecing together Misty Vanderlin's movements on the day of the murder.

"She's the most dedicated curator we've ever had," said the elderly docent in Archives.

"Completely transformed our Modern wing," added an assistant in Administration.

"I just can't believe she'd hurt anyone," whispered a young intern, before quickly adding, "but the security footage doesn't lie, does it?"

This sentiment echoed through every conversation. No one wanted to believe she could be guilty, but in the end, they accepted the police narrative. By noon, Lee had filled three pages with notes but found nothing to contradict the official timeline. With a sigh, he headed toward the loading dock at the rear of the museum.

Wooden crates were stacked against the walls in the receiving area, and workers in white gloves carefully unpacked what appeared to be bronze sculptures. A burly man with salt-and-pepper hair directed the operation with the precision of an orchestra conductor.

"Paul Zabala?" Lee approached, extending his hand. "Lee Stewart. I'm looking into the Vanderlin case."

Zabala's eyes lit up at the mention of Misty's name. "Terrible business. Just terrible. Mrs. Vanderlin is an absolute professional. There must be some mistake!"

"Mind if I ask you some questions about last Friday?" Lee gestured to a small office overlooking the loading area.

"Whatever helps Mrs. Vanderlin. She's been nothing but kind to all of us here."

Inside, Zabala cleared a stack of paperwork from a chair. "You know, the logistics of fine art shipping is an art itself."

"I reckon you see a lot of valuable art come through these doors," Lee said, settling into the chair.

"You have no idea." Zabala slapped his knee. "Just last month, we received a Monet worth more than this building. The insurance paperwork alone took three days."

"I imagine there's quite a process."

Zabala straightened, clearly in his element. "First, we coordinate with specialized art handlers. Regular shipping companies won't touch these pieces."

"Makes sense." Lee nodded. "Reckon FedEx can't handle a Rembrandt."

"Exactly. These handlers use climate-controlled vehicles, sometimes even armed guards for the highest-value pieces." Zabala gestured toward a large wooden crate. "Then there's the packaging. Custom crates built to the exact specifications of each piece. Double-walled, acid-free materials, foam inserts molded precisely to the artwork's dimensions."

"Sounds expensive."

"The crating for a major exhibition can run into six figures." Zabala leaned forward. "But the real complexity is in the insurance. Every piece has to be covered door-to-door, with specific riders for transit, handling, and exhibition. The policies even specify acceptable humidity levels."

Lee's eyebrows raised. "That's mighty particular."

"It has to be. We just sent a collection of Degas bronzes to Chicago last week. Twenty million in value, and I personally oversaw every aspect of the packing. The Smithsonian is getting our Dutch Masters next month." Pride filled Zabala's voice. "Mrs. Vanderlin trusts me with the logistics for all our outgoing exhibitions."

"Speaking of Mrs. Vanderlin," Lee redirected gently, "I understand she spent most of last Friday here in shipping?"

Zabala nodded eagerly. "All day, practically. We had several important arrivals for the Baroque exhibition. The same one where ..." his voice trailed off.

"Where her husband was found," Lee finished. "Can you verify her timeline for Friday?"

"Absolutely. She arrived around nine, checked in with me about some crating requirements." Zabala pulled out a clipboard. "She was in and out all day. Supervising unpacking, signing documentation, discussing placement with the installation team."

"Was she ever gone for extended periods?"

"Just lunch. Maybe ninety minutes. Otherwise, she was never away for more than twenty minutes at a stretch." Zabala's brow furrowed. "There were at least four of us here who could confirm that. We're racing against the clock to finish installation before the opening this weekend." A cloud crossed his face. "I wonder if the opening will be delayed now."

Lee jotted notes. "Y'all work closely with Mrs. Vanderlin, I take it?"

"For seven years now." Something wistful crossed Zabala's face. "She's the most knowledgeable curator I've ever worked with. Treats even the maintenance staff with respect."

"No conflicts? Disagreements about exhibitions?"

"Never." Zabala's answer came too quickly. "Well, nothing serious. Just the usual artistic differences."

Lee looked up from his notepad, watching Zabala's eyes dart toward Misty's office. "You seem to think highly of her."

A flush crept up Zabala's neck. "Everyone does. Ask anyone in this building. Misty Vanderlin is incapable of violence."

"What about her husband? Did you know him well?"

"James?" Zabala's expression cooled. "He came to openings, fundraisers. Always charming, always perfect. The ideal museum benefactor."

"But?" Lee pressed.

"But nothing." Zabala stood abruptly. "I should get back to the unpacking. The interim curator will be looking for these condition reports."

As Lee walked toward the exit, he paused to study a shipping manifest left on a counter. The signature at the bottom matched the example he had for Misty Vanderlin. Time-stamped 5:37 PM last Friday—less than four hours before her husband's murder.

Sammi tapped rhythmically at her keyboard as she updated a case file. The office was quiet except for the occasional clink from the radiator. Three hours of administrative work had left her restless, but she wasn't in the mood to listen to music. Her mind kept repeating the same questions. Who is Gavin Tucker? How did camera twelve go down at the exact moment when

Misty left the room? Where was Christopher Euler getting mysterious cash payments?

The door opened, and Jake walked in. He hung his jacket and headed to the coffeepot.

"Hey, Jakey!" Sammi spun her chair to face him. "How'd it go with Mr. Fancy CEO?"

"Lacroix was ..." Jake paused, filling his coffee cup, "less than forthcoming about his business." He dropped a manila folder on her desk. "But his secretary was more helpful."

Sammi flipped through the documents, excitement building. "Financial records! Did you charm these out of her, or—"

"Let's just say I appealed to her sense of justice." Jake checked his watch. "We've got a few hours before our meeting with Margaret this afternoon. How about we hit the gym? You're overdue for some self-defense training."

Sammi jumped up, grateful for the chance to move. "Seriously? You're finally going to teach me some of your super-secret NSA combat tricks?"

"Basic defensive techniques," Jake corrected, smiling. "If you're serious about this line of work, you need to know how to protect yourself."

Thirty minutes later, they stood in the center of Upton Boxing Center, a no-frills gym with peeling paint and the permanent scent of sweat. They had both changed into workout clothes and found a quiet corner.

"First rule," Jake demonstrated a ready stance, hands raised, "your best defense is awareness. Most attackers rely on surprise."

Sammi mirrored his position, bouncing slightly on her toes. "Got it. Constant vigilance and all that, right?"

"This isn't Harry Potter," Jake said dryly. "It's about recognizing threatening behavior before it escalates."

For the next hour, Jake walked her through basic defensive moves—how to break a wrist grab, escape a chokehold, and create distance from an attacker. Sammi picked up the techniques quickly.

"Not bad," Jake said after she successfully executed a palm-heel strike against the pad he held. "You've done this before."

"Mi abuela made sure all her granddaughters knew how to throw a punch." Breathing hard, Sammi wiped sweat from her forehead. "But nothing structured like this."

Jake nodded approvingly. "Your grandmother sounds like a wise woman."

"She was," Sammi said, breathing heavily. "Growing up in Aguadilla, she thought self-defense was as important as good manners."

"Smart lady." Jake, infuriatingly, looked barely winded.

"How are you not exhausted?" she complained, gulping water. "You're like, twenty years older than me!"

Jake's eyes crinkled at the corners. "Twenty-two, actually. And I've been doing this since before you were born."

"Show-off." Sammi threw her towel at him. "I'm starving. Feed me or I'll practice that wrist lock on you."

"I'm terrified," Jake deadpanned. "There's a decent diner two blocks from here."

They gathered their gear and pushed through the gym's heavy door into the cold afternoon. Jake's Jeep was parked at the curb, and leaning against it was a trim man with jet black hair in an immaculate charcoal suit, aviator sunglasses hiding his eyes.

Jake's posture shifted ever so slightly—shoulders squaring, steps lengthening. He moved in front of Sammi, a protective gesture that made her pulse race.

"Chen," Jake acknowledged, his voice dropping to a lower register. "Didn't know you were in town."

The man removed his sunglasses, revealing shrewd eyes that assessed Sammi before returning to Jake. "She's a little young for you, isn't she, Mercer?"

Jake's jaw tightened. "She's my colleague. What do you want?"

Sammi stayed quiet. It didn't take intelligence training to sense the tension between the men. Her gaze bounced between them as they spoke.

"What were you doing talking to Owen Lacroix?" Chen asked, straightening from the car.

"Client confidentiality," Jake replied. "Why is the FBI interested?"

Chen's expression remained neutral. "Economic Espionage Unit has concerns about certain financial activities at Meridian Tech. Activities that might connect to your client's dead husband."

Sammi's eyes widened. She bit her lip to keep from interrupting.

Jake crossed his arms. "We were just heading to lunch. If you want to tell us about these 'concerns,' you're welcome to join us."

Chen hesitated, clearly reluctant to share information. "This isn't a social call, Mercer."

"Never is with you." Jake walked past the man and opened the door of his Jeep, waving for Sammi to get inside. He spoke over his shoulder to Chen, who hadn't moved. "But I know that look. You need something from us, which means you'll have to give a little to get a little."

After a moment's consideration, Chen nodded curtly. "Twenty minutes. That's all I'm giving you."

14

Katherine parked her silver sedan in the visitor's lot of the Walters Art Museum, her mind still half-focused on the conversation she had just had with Dr. Emily Reed. It had been hard to meet with a psychologist. Harder still to admit that after eight years, she still felt disconnected. From herself, from her purpose. The cold breeze nipped at her cheeks as she approached the imposing building.

Inside, the museum's grand foyer welcomed her with its marble columns and hushed atmosphere. Katherine paused to look at a small oil painting depicting a stormy seascape, the artist's brushstrokes capturing the tumultuous waves with remarkable precision. Art had once been her refuge. A refuge she shared with Daniel. Eight years had done nothing to dull her grief. And her connection to the intelligence community ...

She tore her eyes from the painting and checked her BlackBerry. No messages from Lee. With a sigh, she dialed his number, unsurprised when it went straight to voicemail.

"Still using that dinosaur of a phone," she murmured, slipping her own device back into her pocket. Lee's ancient flip phone was notorious for its poor reception, especially in buildings with thick stone walls.

Katherine made her way toward the offices, her footsteps echoing on the polished floor. The hallway was lined with photographs of past exhibitions, a visual timeline of the museum's history.

The administrative wing was quieter than she expected. Most offices stood empty, their occupants likely avoiding the scene of James Vanderlin's death. As she passed the curator's suite, movement caught her eye.

Beth Taylor sat at Misty's desk, rearranging folders.

Katherine paused in the doorway. Their interview yesterday had been uncomfortably revealing. Beth had made good on her threat to tell the police about her affair and her pregnancy, which gave the prosecutor the motive they were looking for.

"Ms. Taylor," Katherine said. "I'm surprised to see you here."

The younger woman startled, her hand flying to her chest. "Ms. Carson! I didn't hear you come in."

Katherine stepped into the office. "I didn't expect to see you here today."

"Someone has to take up the slack." Beth's voice was clipped as she straightened a stack of catalogs. "The exhibition opens in three days. The board has asked me to step in as interim curator."

"Congratulations on the promotion," Katherine said, the words deliberately neutral.

Beth's eyes narrowed slightly. "I earned it. Three years of working in Misty's shadow, handling the real work while she got the credit."

"I'm surprised the board didn't postpone the opening, considering the circumstances."

"Art waits for no one, Ms. Carson." Beth's smile didn't reach her eyes. "Not even murder." She stood abruptly. "I need to check on a shipment in receiving. You can come with me if you'd like. I believe your colleague is there speaking with Mr. Zabala."

Katherine followed Beth through the labyrinthine corridors, noting how the new interim curator walked with confidence, her heels clicking sharply against the floor. For someone who had discovered a murdered man less than a week ago, Beth seemed remarkably composed. Almost too composed.

"It must be difficult," Katherine said, "being in the same space where you found him."

"We all process trauma differently, Ms. Carson."

Katherine nodded. "When we spoke at your apartment, you mentioned your relationship with James began six months ago. That would be around the time of the summer fundraiser, correct?"

Beth missed a step, her composure slipping. "You've been investigating me."

"I investigate everyone connected to my cases," Katherine replied calmly. "Especially those who change their stories."

"I haven't changed anything." Beth's voice took on a defensive edge.

"The innocent witness at the crime scene. The grieving lover at your apartment. Today, the capable professional who is glad to be out of Misty's shadow." Katherine kept her tone even, watching as Beth's hand tightened around her key card. "Competing narratives make me curious."

Beth's face flushed as they reached the heavy metal door to the shipping department. She swiped her key card with trembling fingers and avoided Katherine's gaze.

"You don't know anything about me," she whispered, the words barely audible as the door swung open.

The shipping department was a vast concrete-floored space filled with shelving units and work tables. Beth scanned the room, her lips pursed.

"Mr. Zabala should be here," she said, checking her watch. "He must be in the secondary vault. I need to speak with him immediately." She pointed toward the far side of the room. "Your colleague is over there. Excuse me."

Beth strode away, disappearing through a door marked "Authorized Personnel Only" before Katherine could respond.

Katherine made her way across the warehouse floor, navigating between stacks of empty crates and packing materials. She spotted Lee examining a shipping manifest near a row of recently unpacked sculptures.

Katherine made her way to him. "I see you've made yourself at home."

"This place is a gold mine of information," Lee whispered. "Zabala confirms Misty's timeline for Friday. She was here most of the day, visible to multiple staff members."

"Margaret met with the prosecutor last night," Katherine replied, keeping her voice down. "They're offering a plea deal: second-degree murder, fifteen years."

Lee whistled softly. "Sounds like they are worried about their case."

Katherine shook her head. "I think they just aren't interested in proving premeditation."

"Hard to prove premeditation if our client is innocent. And I think I've come up with another possibility for us to—"

A sharp metallic groan cut through their conversation. Katherine turned toward the sound. A stack of empty packing crates on a rolling cart swayed precariously.

"That doesn't look right," Lee said, his voice suddenly tense.

The cart tilted, seeming to hesitate for a moment before gathering momentum. The topmost crates began to slide.

"Move!" Katherine shouted, grabbing Lee's arm and pulling him sideways as the first crate crashed to the floor.

The impact sent the empty wooden box splintering across the concrete, triggering a chain reaction. The cart toppled completely, sending the remaining crates tumbling in a thunderous cascade directly where they had been standing.

One large crate caught the edge of a metal shelving unit as it fell, causing the entire structure to sway dangerously. The shelf was stacked with lightweight foam packing materials and empty conservation supplies.

Katherine and Lee pressed themselves against the concrete support pillar as packing materials rained down around them. A small wooden box fell on Katherine's head. Foam peanuts floated through the air like bizarre snowflakes, settling on their shoulders and hair.

For three heartbeats, there was perfect silence. Then chaos erupted.

Alarms blared and footsteps pounded as workers rushed into the room.

"You okay?" Lee asked, his voice husky with adrenaline.

Katherine nodded, raising her hand to her forehead. "Just a few scrapes." Her gaze swept the room. The damage was substantial. Empty crates and packing materials destroyed, but not a single artwork harmed.

The "Authorized Personnel" door burst open. Paul Zabala rushed in. "What happened?" he shouted, surveying the destruction. "The security system just triggered!"

Katherine watched him carefully. His surprise seemed genuine, but something in his eyes, perhaps a flicker of relief when he saw the undamaged artwork, raised her suspicions.

"Cart collapsed," Lee said calmly, brushing foam peanuts from his shirt. "Restraining bracket appears to have failed."

Zabala moved closer, examining the wreckage. "That's impossible. I secured those carts myself this morning."

Katherine bent down, picking up a metal pin that should have secured the bracket to the wall. She held it up. "This didn't fall out on its own."

Zabala's expression darkened. "We should review the security footage immediately."

Beth appeared in the doorway, her face pale. "Is anyone hurt?" Her eyes darted around the room, lingering on Katherine and Lee before shifting to the undamaged artwork nearby.

"Just missed us," Katherine said. "Fortunate that no valuable pieces were damaged."

"Very fortunate," Beth agreed, her voice steady.

Katherine slipped the metal pin into her pocket. Someone had deliberately targeted them. And whoever it was knew enough about the museum's shipping procedures to stage an "accident" that would threaten them without risking the valuable artwork.

"You know what they say about coincidences in murder investigations," she muttered to Lee as museum staff began clearing the debris.

Lee nodded, his eyes tracking both Beth and Zabala as they conferred in hushed tones across the room. "I don't believe in 'em either."

15

The diner smelled like coffee and grease, a comforting contrast to the stiffness radiating from FBI Agent Chen. Sammi slid into the vinyl booth next to Jake, trying not to feel like a kid at the adults' table. Jake's posture was casual, but she'd been around him long enough now to recognize the set of his jaw that signaled heightened alertness.

Chen removed his sunglasses, folding them carefully before setting them on the table. "Twenty minutes," he reminded them, checking his watch. "That's all."

The waitress appeared, her smile fading when she caught the atmosphere at their table. Jake ordered black coffee, Chen requested water, and Sammi asked for a chocolate milkshake, ignoring Chen's look of disdain.

"So," Jake leaned forward, "what's the Economic Espionage Unit doing sniffing around Meridian Tech?"

Chen's rapped the table with his knuckles. "The DOJ has concerns about certain intellectual property transfers."

"FARA violations?" Jake asked.

Chen's gaze slid to Sammi. "Not directly. More CFIUS jurisdiction with potential IEEPA implications."

Sammi kept quiet despite her growing frustration. She recognized FARA from a college paper. Foreign Agents Registration Act. But CFIUS? IEEPA? She'd have to look those up later. The acronyms flew between them like coded messages, and she wondered if Jake was deliberately using them to make Chen feel comfortable, speaking a language that excluded her.

"The Bureau looking at Section 1831 charges?" Jake's voice remained conversational, but Sammi caught the slight edge.

Chen's mouth tightened. "I'm not at liberty to discuss specific statutes under consideration."

"But you think James Vanderlin was involved." Jake made it a statement, not a question.

"We had him under observation." Chen's admission came reluctantly. "His department financial activities showed unusual patterns."

"Such as?" Jake pressed.

"Irregular wire transfers. Consultancy payments to shell companies that—" He stopped abruptly, as if remembering Sammi was there. "That raised red flags."

The waitress returned with their drinks. Sammi wrapped her hands around the cold milkshake glass, using the moment of silence to study Chen. His suit was expensive but conservative, his haircut military-precise. Nothing like the rumpled FBI agents she'd seen in movies.

"What makes you think our client is connected?" Jake asked after the waitress left.

"Mrs. Vanderlin's position at the museum creates opportunities for NSPA concerns intertwined with our investigation."

NSPA. Sammi frantically searched her memory. National... something... Property Act? She wasn't sure.

"The Walters Museum has significant international loans," Chen continued, looking only at Jake. "Perfect cover for certain ... transactions."

Jake's eyebrows lifted. "You're suggesting art smuggling as a front?"

"I'm not suggesting anything specific." Chen took a careful sip of water. "But when a tech executive with classified clearance ends up dead in his wife's museum, certain dots connect themselves."

Sammi felt her breath catch. Classified clearance? Nobody had mentioned that about James Vanderlin before. She forced herself to sip her milkshake, trying to appear unfazed while her mind raced.

"What about Owen Lacroix?" Jake asked. "How deep does his involvement go?"

Chen's expression tightened. "Meridian Tech has defense contracts that touch sensitive areas. Lacroix meets regularly with a cultural attaché from ..." his eyes flicked to Sammi again, "... a nation of interest."

Sammi realized that Chen kept pausing whenever he remembered she was there. It was infuriating. But also revealing. Whatever they were talking about was way bigger than just some rich guy getting killed at a museum.

"HUMINT or SIGINT leading your investigation?" Jake's question made Chen visibly tense.

"I'm not at liberty to disclose that, Mercer."

Jake smiled thinly. "But you need something from us, or you wouldn't be here."

The diner door chimed, and Chen shifted slightly, scanning the new arrivals before returning his attention to Jake. The move was so subtle, so automatic, that Sammi might have missed it if she weren't watching closely.

"What I need," Chen said carefully, "is to know what Vanderlin told his wife about Meridian's quantum encryption project."

Jake's expression didn't change, but Sammi felt the air between them shift. Quantum encryption. That, at least, she understood from her cybersecurity classes.

"Our client hasn't mentioned any encryption projects," Jake said. "She claims she and her husband kept their work lives separate."

"SAP protocols would require it," Chen nodded, "but pillow talk happens."

SAP. Special Access Programs? Sammi remembered that from a documentary about military secrets. This was definitely above her security clearance, if she had one. Which she didn't.

"We'll ask," Jake promised, "discreetly. But you need to give us more to work with. Misty Vanderlin is facing murder charges."

Agent Chen leaned back, studying Jake. "Let's just say certain foreign entities would pay handsomely for what Meridian Tech is developing. If Vanderlin was selling secrets ..."

"Then there's a whole new set of suspects," Sammi interjected, unable to contain herself.

Both men turned to look at her. Jake with a hint of approval, Chen with barely disguised annoyance.

"Intelligence matters are complicated, Miss Garcia." Chen's tone was dismissive. "There are layers of—"

"She's right," Jake cut in. "If James was involved in espionage, that creates motives beyond a jealous wife. Gives us somewhere to look."

"I've already said more than I should." Chen stood, straightening his suit jacket. "Our conversation never happened. If anyone asks, we discussed witness protection options for Mrs. Vanderlin." He paused, looking directly at Sammi for the first time. "Be careful, Ms. Garcia. This case isn't a good training ground."

After he left, Sammi released a breath. "Wow. He's intense."

Jake sipped his coffee, eyes watching Chen through the window as he walked to a nondescript sedan. "Chen's a good agent. By-the-book, but smart."

"Was all that ... real?" Sammi asked quietly. "Or was he fishing?"

"Both." Jake's answer was immediate. "He gave us just enough to point us in a direction, while trying to see what we know." He studied her face. "How much did you follow?"

Sammi straightened her shoulders. "Not everything. But enough to know we're dealing with something way bigger than a cheating husband getting shot." She hesitated. "This is way above my training, isn't it?"

Jake's expression softened. "No one's ever fully trained for cases like this, Sammi. I've been doing this for decades, and I still get blindsided."

The casual admission from someone as capable as Jake was both terrifying and oddly comforting.

16

Katherine winced as the antiseptic stung the small cut above her eyebrow. The warehouse incident had left her with a few scrapes, and the suspicious timing hadn't escaped her notice.

"Hold still," Jake instructed, placing a bandage on the wound.

The Carson Investigations office hummed with activity as the team gathered for their meeting with Margaret Mitchell. Lee brewed fresh coffee, the rich aroma filling the room. Sammi was busy updating the notes on their investigation board.

Margaret came in with a bright, "Hi, all!" Her gaze fell on Katherine's injury. "Good Lord, hon, what happened to you?"

Katherine waved away the concern. "Nothing serious."

"Nothing serious?" Lee laughed. "Nearly got buried under a pile of empty boxes and shipping materials that 'accidentally' came loose right where we were standing."

"What?" Margaret exclaimed. "Tell me everything!" She settled onto the couch while Lee shared the details.

Katherine grimaced. "And they were careful. Not a single piece of artwork was damaged."

Margaret's brow furrowed. "Well, I know you all can handle yourselves. But it seems someone is testing your reflexes."

"Let's focus on what we know first," Katherine said, shifting into manager mode. "Something bigger is happening here, and James Vanderlin was in the middle of it."

Jake cleared his throat. "Sammi and I have some information that might explain a few things." He nodded at the youngest team member. "Sammi, show them what you found."

Sammi straightened, tucking a strand of dark hair behind her ear. "Well, this morning I was researching the artwork in the gallery where James was killed. The centerpiece was a Baroque painting called Judith beheading Holofernes by Trophime Bigot." She pinned an image to the board—a dramatic scene of a woman cutting off a general's head. "According to Jewish history, Judith was a widow who saved her people by seducing an enemy general, getting him drunk, and beheading him."

"The police think it might be a message," Katherine added. "A woman's victory over a powerful man."

"That's quite the symbolism," Margaret mused, leaning forward. "But is it a coincidence, or did someone deliberately choose that location?"

"Nothing about this murder seems coincidental," Katherine said. "The expert shot, the perfect framing of Misty, the gallery location ... it's all too clean."

"Speaking of clean," Jake interjected, "we crossed paths with someone interesting today. Agent Chen from the FBI's Economic Espionage Unit."

The room fell silent.

Jake continued, resting his hands on his knees. "Meridian Tech is under federal investigation for corporate espionage and intellectual property theft. The DOJ is concerned because of their government contracts."

"That explains why Owen Lacroix was so evasive during your interview," Katherine said.

"Exactly," Jake confirmed. "Chen wouldn't give us much, but it's clear they suspect someone at Meridian Tech has been selling trade secrets. James might have discovered something, or he could have been involved. He told Lacroix he was working on a project that would 'change everything'."

Lee tapped a pen against his notepad. "So we've got a murder that looks personal but might be professional. The question is: who benefits from James being dead?"

"Let's run through our suspects," Katherine suggested, moving to the board. "Anna Bovill."

Lee nodded, his expression thoughtful. "She's definitely hiding something. They were high school sweethearts, and I got the impression there were unresolved feelings. Her relationship with Kyle seems ... awkward." He took a swig of his coffee.

Jake spoke up. "Lacroix mentioned that Anna and James had a strange dynamic. He couldn't understand why she stayed working for him all these years." He set his mug on the coffee table. "The manager at the gun club said James was teaching his female assistant to shoot," he added. "But Anna denied it."

"Okay." Katherine turned back to the board. "Next suspect: Owen Lacroix."

Jake shrugged. "Could be that his evasiveness was solely due to the FBI investigation. But if James discovered something incriminating at Meridian Tech ... Who knows?"

"Beth Taylor is also very suspicious. She was in the shipping area when the incident occurred." Katherine moved to sit on the couch with the others.

Jake shifted to make room. "We learned from Mr. Harwick that Beth may have influenced James's decision to investigate the authenticity of a certain piece of artwork. He gave us the name of the conservationist that James was working with."

"Right. I also think she got back to work awfully fast for someone whose lover was just killed." Katherine made eye contact with Margaret. "The police have evidence that Misty knew about the affair."

Margaret's mouth opened. "No, it can't be."

"Someone told her at a Halloween party last year. And she made a scene."

Margaret closed her eyes and looked down at her hands.

"What about the shipping director?" Lee asked. "Paul Zabala seemed protective of Misty, and he could have arranged our little accident."

Katherine wrote Zabala's name on a card and pinned it to the board. "But if he's infatuated with Misty, why would he want to frame her for murder?"

Jake said, "Maybe so he could be her knight in shining armor. Helping prove her innocence. Stepping in when she's vulnerable."

"That's twisted," Sammi muttered.

"Murder usually is," Katherine said.

Margaret cleared her throat. "I confirmed that Misty did change her dentist appointment last Friday, just as she told us. But..." She hesitated, her expression troubled. "I've known Misty since college. She's always been passionate, intense even. There was this one time in our junior year. A professor accused her of plagiarism. It wasn't true, but Misty ..." She shook her head. "I've never seen anyone so angry. She threatened him right there in front of everyone. Said she'd make him regret it. The next day, all his research files were deleted from the university server."

Katherine raised her eyebrows. "You think she did it?"

"She never admitted it," Margaret replied. "But she had the computer skills. And the temper." She sighed. "I want to believe in my friend, I do. But I'm starting to have doubts."

"No, Maggie," Jake said gently. "Clean headshot, perfect execution. Not the kind of shot most civilians make, especially in a panic."

"Right," Katherine agreed. "Even if she had motive and opportunity, that wasn't a crime of passion. It was calculated."

"I know. That's what worries me. What if there's more to Misty than I know?"

"We need to consider the physical aspects of this crime. Misty is five-foot-three and slight. James was a former football player who still worked out regularly. How could she have moved his body under that display table by herself?" Katherine asked.

"Yeah," Margaret replied softly. "But you still haven't figured out how Misty's gun got to the crime scene if she didn't take it there."

"Not yet," Jake said, "but don't give up hope."

"What about Gavin?" Lee spoke up. "The technician who installed the security cameras?"

"The security system James donated to the museum?" Katherine asked.

"According to Frank Naylor and the volunteers, Gavin was at the museum every day the week before the murder," Lee added. "I've been trying to call him, but haven't got an answer so far."

Sammi spoke up. "According to his Facebook page, Gavin Tucker is somewhere in D.C. this week."

"That's what Naylor told me," Lee confirmed.

Katherine nodded. "That security system was installed to coincide with the opening of this new exhibit, wasn't it?"

"Yes," Lee confirmed. "And there's something else. With this Gavin out of town, the system hasn't been inspected yet."

"Convenient timing," Katherine said, thoughtfully.

Margaret leaned forward. "You think that's connected to the murder?"

"I don't know," Katherine admitted. "But ... It feels like we're looking at pieces of the same puzzle."

"What's our next step?" Lee glanced at the board.

"We need to talk to Misty about the affair," Katherine said firmly. "And the baby. She deserves to know what we've learned."

Margaret winced. "I'm not looking forward to that conversation."

"We need to know what she knew and when," Katherine insisted. "If James was having one affair with Beth, he could've been having others. Possibly with Anna."

"We'll talk to her tomorrow," Margaret promised. "But tread carefully. Misty's in a fragile state, denied bail and sitting in a cell for a murder I still hope she didn't commit." She looked sideways at Jake when she said "hope" and blushed when he met her gaze.

Katherine and Lee exchanged a knowing look. They were both getting impatient for Jake to get his act together and ask Margaret out.

Katherine nodded, moving on with the assignments. "We need to split up. Jake, see if you can find out what James was working on with Dr. Volkov. Lee, you head to SecureTech Solutions to track down this Gavin character. I'm headed back to the museum to figure out how Misty's cell phone sent messages without her knowing about it."

Lee inclined his head toward Sammi, who had been quietly taking notes. "That leaves us with confirming whether Anna Bovill was at the gun range."

Katherine considered for a moment. "Sammi, how would you feel about handling that on your own? Take Anna's photo to the gun club manager. See if he identifies her as the woman James was teaching to shoot."

Sammi's eyes widened, her pen freezing mid-note. "Me? Solo? As in, my first real field assignment?"

She took the photo of Anna that Lee extended to her. "I know this is necessary, but ... it feels weird, you know? Anna has no idea we're investigating her private life. What if she was just learning to protect herself after that break-in?"

Katherine's expression grew more serious. "Those feelings you're having? Don't lose them. The day this work stops bothering you is the day you should find a different job." She leaned forward. "But Sammi, someone murdered James Vanderlin and framed Misty for it. Anna might be innocent, or she might be the key to freeing our client. We can't know without asking the right questions."

"And it's a straightforward identification task," Jake chimed in. "Perfect for your first time out alone. Remember that we're not trying to destroy Anna's life. We're trying to find the truth."

Sammi nodded slowly, tucking the photo into her folder. "The truth. Right. Even when it's uncomfortable to find." She looked back to Katherine. "I won't let you down."

Katherine smiled. "I know you won't."

Margaret gathered her things and gave Katherine a light hug. "I just hope I still know who Misty is," she whispered.

Katherine understood the feeling all too well. People weren't always who you thought they were. She'd learned that lesson the hard way. But somewhere in this tangle of lies, affairs, and corporate espionage was the truth about who killed James Vanderlin.

And they were getting closer.

17

Sammi hung back while Jake and Lee were heading out on their assignments. She needed to talk to Katherine alone.

"Good luck on your assignment, Sammi," Margaret Mitchell smiled warmly at her as she left the room. "You're doing great."

"Thanks, Professor Mitch—I mean Margaret." Sammi hadn't gotten used to calling her former college professor by her first name. Margaret had introduced her to Katherine a couple years ago which led to this job opportunity.

"Um, Katherine?" Sammi asked once they were alone. "I know this murder case is really important, but ..."

Katherine stood. "Do you have something on the Hackett case?"

Sammi breathed a sigh of relief. "Yeah, I do."

"Great," Katherine said, moving to the desk she shared with Lee. She opened the top file drawer and pulled out a blue file folder.

Sammi's lips parted in surprise. "You remembered. With everything going on, I thought ..."

Katherine sat on the edge of the desk. "No case is too small, chica. What did you find?"

Sammi beamed. "I ran his background this morning. Clean record, steady employment history at Mason & Blackwell for five years." She spoke faster as she gained confidence. "His social media presence is practically non-existent. LinkedIn shows his work history, and Facebook hasn't been updated in eight months. I found him on a classic car forum and a fantasy football league using the username Cynthia gave us, but nothing suspicious."

Katherine tilted her head. "Nothing suspicious, or too clean?"

"That's what I was thinking. Guy his age with his interests usually leaves more of a digital footprint. It's like he's being deliberately careful about what he shares online."

Katherine pulled a printout from the folder. "I followed up on those deposits Cynthia mentioned. Christopher's been making regular deposits—always in cash, always on Wednesdays, always between $800 and $1,200."

"Wow!" Sammi exclaimed. "How long has that been going on?"

"Six months or longer. That's as far back as Cynthia could get copies of his bank statements without him knowing. His annual salary is $68,000, and he gets paid on Fridays. But the cash deposits add up to over $20,000."

"That's a significant side hustle."

"So, what's our next step?" Katherine asked.

Sammi's eyes lit up. "You want me to come up with the plan?"

"Your instincts brought us this far." Katherine closed the file and leaned back against the desk. "What does your gut tell you?"

Sammi paced a few steps, her mind racing. "We need to find out where that extra cash is coming from. If Christopher's involved in something shady, his employer might know about it—or be part of it."

"Good. And how do we approach Mason & Blackwell without alerting them that Christopher's under investigation?"

"We go in through the back door. You pose as a potential client. Feel them out about ... I don't know, services they might offer that aren't exactly advertised?"

Katherine's lips curved into a smile. "Not bad, Garcia. Not bad at all."

The offices of Mason & Blackwell occupied the third floor of a renovated brick building near Inner Harbor. Katherine had chosen her outfit carefully. A charcoal business suit with a silk blouse, expensive enough to suggest serious money, but conservative enough to blend in. Her heels clicked purposefully across the polished marble lobby.

The receptionist, a young woman with perfectly styled blonde hair, looked up with a practiced smile. "Good afternoon. How may I help you?"

"I have an appointment with Christopher Euler." Katherine's voice carried the crisp authority of someone accustomed to being taken seriously. "Samantha Casey."

She'd used Sammi's first name, which made her apprentice smile, and a classic moniker that made her smile. "K.C." Katherine Carson.

"Of course, Ms. Casey. Mr. Euler is expecting you."

Christopher Euler's office was a large, well-lit room in the back of the building. He didn't have a window, but three large landscape paintings hung along the back wall. The man himself was in his early fifties, with a receding hairline and hunched posture that was only magnified by his dark suit and striped bowtie.

"Ms. Casey." He stood, extending his hand. "Please, have a seat. Coffee? Water?"

"Water would be fine." Katherine settled into the client chair.

He pressed his intercom. "Melissa? Two waters, please."

"So," Euler returned to his chair, folding his hands on the desk, "you mentioned on the phone that you're looking for discretionary financial services. Tell me more about your situation."

Katherine had rehearsed this part during the drive over. "My late husband left me with significant assets, but some of them are ... complicated. I need someone who understands that not every transaction needs to be documented in excruciating detail."

Euler's expression didn't change, but he shifted slightly forward. "I see. What kind of complications are we discussing?"

"The kind that require flexible accounting. Cash transactions that need to be managed carefully." Katherine paused as the receptionist brought in their water. "I was told you might be able to help with such arrangements."

"May I ask who referred you?"

"A mutual acquaintance. Someone who values discretion as much as I do." Katherine sipped her water, maintaining eye contact. "They mentioned you'd recently expanded your services in this area."

Euler set down his glass with deliberate care. "Ms. Casey, I want to be clear about something. Mason & Blackwell operates within all legal boundaries. We provide legitimate financial consulting services."

"Of course." Katherine's tone remained neutral. "I would expect nothing less from a firm of your reputation."

"That said," Euler continued, his voice dropping, "we do understand that our clients sometimes have unique needs. Complex estate planning, international transactions, private investment opportunities."

"Such as?"

"Well, for instance, we might help facilitate cash-based business transactions for clients who prefer to maintain privacy in their dealings. Nothing illegal, you understand, but perhaps something that does not need to be ... prominently featured in standard financial reports."

Katherine nodded slowly. "I see. And this is something you've been doing long?"

"Actually, I handle this particular aspect of our services personally. My former associate, Harold Cartwright, handled these matters until his retirement last year." Euler's smile had a predatory edge. "But I've taken over completely."

"I'd like to know more about how this works." Katherine leaned forward. "Perhaps you could explain the process? I need someone with experience in these arrangements."

Euler glanced toward his office door, then leaned back in his chair. "The process is quite simple, really. Clients bring cash to me directly at an offsite location. I handle the conversion into legitimate business transactions through our various accounts." He paused, studying Katherine's face. "Small amounts, of course. Nothing that would raise flags. Processed through different channels each time."

"And the documentation?"

"Minimal paperwork. Everything appears as consulting fees or investment advisory services. Clean, simple, and completely legitimate on paper." Euler's fingers drummed lightly on his desk. "Harold taught me well before he left."

Katherine maintained her interested expression. "That sounds exactly like what I need. Very professional."

Euler stood, signaling the meeting's end. "I think you'll find our services exactly what you're looking for, Ms. Casey. When you're ready to begin, just call and ask for me specifically."

Katherine rose as well, extending her hand. "Thank you, Mr. Euler. This has been most enlightening."

"My pleasure, Ms. Casey. I look forward to working with you."

As Katherine walked back to her car, she pulled out her phone and dialed Sammi's number.

"Hello?"

"It's Katherine. You were right about going in through the back door. Christopher Euler isn't just taking money under the table. He's helping them launder it."

18

SecureTech Solutions occupied a sleek storefront in a modern strip mall on the outskirts of Baltimore. The company's polished exterior, with its high-tech display windows and digital signage, showcased the ambition of its owner despite being only ten years in business. Lee entered confidently, ID already in hand.

"I'm Lee Stewart, a private detective," he said to the receptionist, a young woman with a sleek ponytail, dressed in a blue button-down dress shirt with the company's logo embroidered above the pocket. "I need to speak with Gavin Tucker."

The woman's expression shifted from boredom to alertness. "Mr. Tucker isn't in today. But Mr. Bovill is available. He's the owner and might be able to help you."

Lee's interest piqued. Kyle Bovill—Anna's husband. Another connection to James Vanderlin. "That would be perfect, actually."

"One moment." She picked up her phone, murmured something, then looked back at Lee. "You can wait in the conference room. Second door on the left."

Lee nodded his thanks and made his way down the hallway. The conference room was small but expensively furnished with glass walls, a sleek table, and ergonomic chairs.

The door swung open almost immediately. Mr. Bovill entered with the energy of a minor whirlwind. Today he was dressed in the same uniform as the receptionist, except Kyle's dress shirt was a bit faded with stains on the cuffs. His hands were already in motion, gesturing as he spoke.

"Detective Stewart! From Carson Investigations, right?" His eyes darted around the room. "How can I help? Do you—are you looking at the security footage? Because I'd be happy to assist with any technical aspects you might find confusing."

Lee kept his expression neutral. "I understand one of your technicians, Gavin Tucker, installed the security system at the Walters."

"Correct." Kyle nodded vigorously, his fingers drumming rapidly on the table. "One of my best. Very detail-oriented. The museum installation was perfect, state-of-the-art, cutting edge." He tilted his head. "Why? Is there something wrong with it? You didn't mention any issues with the system yesterday."

"I'm looking into some potential connections," Lee said, deliberately vague. "I was hoping to speak with Mr. Tucker directly."

"Gavin? Oh, he's on vacation this week." Kyle waved dismissively. "In Washington D.C."

"Was this a last-minute trip?" Lee asked casually.

Kyle shook his head, hands animating his response. "Not at all! He's been planning it since the election in November. Very politically involved, our Gavin. He was thrilled when Barack Obama won. Couldn't wait to attend the inauguration festivities."

"I understand he was at the museum quite a bit during the installation."

"Just to set up the equipment," Kyle said with a dismissive wave. "I designed the system myself, exactly to James's specifications. Beautiful system, if I do say so myself. I can get you a copy of the blueprints, if you like?"

"That would be helpful. Do you know who Gavin interacted with at the museum?"

Kyle tapped at his phone for a moment. "Sara at the front desk will have those blueprints ready for you before you leave. Gavin just handled the physical installation—wiring, mounting cameras, that sort of thing. He wouldn't have interacted much with the staff."

"Including Misty Vanderlin?"

"Misty." Kyle's expression softened immediately, his gestures becoming more fluid. "Now there's an extraordinary woman. Brilliant curator. Stunning, isn't she? Way too good for James, if you ask me. Emotional, though. Reacts before she thinks when she's upset. I've seen her at museum events. When something goes wrong, she just ... leaves. Walks away to collect herself."

Lee made a mental note of Kyle's evident admiration. "Did you interact with her much during the installation process?"

"Not as much as I would have liked," Kyle admitted with a rueful smile. He laughed nervously. "I mean, no. Misty didn't know about the new system. It was supposed to be a surprise from James." His eyes took on a distant quality. "She has such vision. James never appreciated what he had."

"I'm investigating the possibility that someone told Misty about her husband's affair."

Kyle's expression shifted, not with surprise but with something more like resignation. "Right. That." He tapped his fingers on the table, his earlier animation subdued.

"You already knew about the affair?" Lee asked.

"Look, James was a great guy. But he was a bit of a jerk sometimes. I couldn't believe it when I found out that he was cheating on her. She's such a beautiful woman." Kyle's voice had softened, almost protective when referring to Misty.

"How long had you known?"

"About six months. Anna found out first—hard not to notice when you're working that closely with someone. She was pretty upset about it." Kyle swallowed. "Not that she had any right to be."

Lee leaned forward. "And did you tell anyone else about it?"

Kyle's gestures stilled, and he looked directly at Lee for the first time. "I told Misty. At a Halloween party last year."

"Why?"

Kyle groaned and seemed to deflate. "I—well—you see—the thing is..." He looked away, then back at Lee. "I know, I know what you're thinking. I'm married too, but Anna has never been happy with me. She always regretted not marrying James. She resents me, and yeah, it made me jealous that she really wanted him, not me."

He stood up, pacing a few steps before continuing. "So I just decided that I was going to put myself out there. I thought if Misty knew about the affair, then she would want to get back at him somehow, and I was just offering my services." A bitter smile crossed his face. "Would have been great if we could have had something, but she rejected me. That's how it goes sometimes."

"Does your wife know about this?" Lee asked, keeping his tone neutral despite his surprise at Kyle's candor.

Kyle scoffed. "Does my wife know that I approached another woman about having an affair? No. I'm not stupid. I didn't think it would ever actually go anywhere, turn into a relationship or anything like that."

He sank back into his chair. "I feel kind of responsible because I'm the one that told Misty about his affair. Was a terrible thing to do. I'm a crappy friend." His voice dropped lower. "I'm not sure if I even really wanted her to have an affair with me. I just wanted her to be angry with James. I wanted somebody to be on my side."

"I understand your wife and James dated in high school."

"Ancient history," Kyle said, but without the animated dismissiveness from earlier. His hands rested limply on the table. "Or so I thought."

"How did Misty react when you told her about the affair?"

Kyle rubbed his temples. "Not how I expected. She was... calm. Too calm. Asked me how I knew for sure. I told her I'd seen the way Beth looked at him, how he always made excuses to stay late when she was working. Plus Anna had confirmed it."

"And then?"

"Well, she didn't run into my arms." Kyle shrugged. "I don't know what I was expecting. She started crying, saying it wasn't true. She ran out of the place and went home. James wasn't there, thank God."

Lee appraised the man carefully. "The night of the murder, where were you?"

"Home. Anna was working late with James. They had to prepare documents for a client presentation. Said James was being extra careful about security protocols lately." He laughed without humor. "Ironic, right? I'm home alone while my wife is with the man she wishes she'd married."

"Your wife was with James on the night he died?" Lee asked, trying to keep any accusation out of his voice.

"Oh, no, no... well, yes. I mean, she worked with him every day. And they did work late that night. But Anna had a fundraising banquet to attend that evening. She would have at least a dozen witnesses."

"Mr. Bovill, do you own a gun?"

Kyle looked genuinely confused by the abrupt question. "No. Why would I? I'm a tech guy. The closest I get to violence is playing *Call of Duty*."

Lee nodded, letting silence fill the room. Kyle seemed exhausted now; the energetic gestures and rapid speech patterns from earlier had stilled.

"Is there anything else you'd like to tell me about James? Anything that might be relevant to the investigation?"

Kyle looked up. "He wasn't perfect, you know. For all his success, all his charm, he took people for granted. Especially the women in his life." He shook his head. "But I never wanted this. Never imagined it would end like this."

The raw emotion in those words struck Lee as genuine. "I'll need to speak with Gavin Tucker when he returns from Washington. And I may have more questions for you."

Kyle nodded. "I understand. I've been ... less than honorable in all this. But I didn't kill James." He met Lee's gaze. "I may have wanted to mess up his marriage, but I didn't want him dead."

As Lee turned to leave, Kyle called after him. "Detective?"

Lee paused at the door.

"When you find who did this—and I hope you do—" Kyle's expression was somber, "let me know. I need to make peace with what I've done."

Outside in the parking lot, Lee pulled out his phone. Katherine answered on the first ring.

"Kat, it's me. Kyle Bovill admits he's the one who told Misty about the affair, but not because he discovered it—because he wanted to start something with her himself."

"Well, that's a development." Katherine's voice was thoughtful. "How'd she take it?"

"Not well."

"I will be asking her about that interaction tomorrow," Katherine said matter-of-factly. "What about Gavin Tucker?"

"Still need to find him. He's supposedly in D.C. for the inauguration, but we should confirm that independently. Kyle might be covering for him."

"Keep digging. If Misty's being framed, someone used that knowledge against her."

"Will do," Lee said. "And Kat? I've got a surprise for you. The blueprints for the Walters' new security system."

19

Sammi hugged herself against the biting wind as she hurried from the bus stop. She could see her breath in the frigid air as she navigated the sidewalk to the Charm City Gun Club. Her heart raced as her boots crunched through patches of dirty snow. Her first solo assignment.

"Just an identification," she murmured to herself, rubbing her gloved hands together. "Straightforward." She stamped her feet at the entrance, shaking off the slush. A bell chimed as she pushed through the door, stepping into the air-conditioned lobby. The place smelled like coffee and ... something burning? *Must be the gunpowder. Do guns still use powder?* Sammi wandered around the lobby for a minute, feeling out of place.

"Help ya?" A man in a faded polo shirt waved from behind the counter. "Todd," according to his name tag.

Sammi stepped up to the counter, working to project confidence. "Hi, I'm Samantha Garcia." She showed her investigator-in-training credentials. "I'm looking into the James Vanderlin case."

Todd adjusted his glasses. "Another one? Your colleague was just here yesterday."

"Jake." Sammi nodded. "I'm following up on something specific." She reached into her folder and pulled out a color printout of Anna Bovill. "We need to confirm if this woman was the guest Mr. Vanderlin brought here."

Todd took the photo and studied it carefully. He frowned. "Hair's similar, but no—this isn't her." He handed the photo back. "The woman James brought had the same coloring, but different face. Thinner nose, higher cheekbones. I'm certain.

Sammi's heart sank as she took the photo back. "You're sure?"

"Been running this place fifteen years. Good with faces." Todd tapped his temple. "Especially regulars. And they were here every Thursday for months."

"I see," Sammi said, trying to hide her disappointment. She tucked the photo away. "Thank you for your time."

She turned to leave, but paused at the door. An idea came to her. She pulled out her phone and opened Facebook, fingers skimming over the screen as she navigated to James Vanderlin's profile. She scrolled through his friends list until she found what she was looking for: Beth Taylor. A brunette woman with business-casual photos and a warm smile.

Sammi pivoted back to Todd. "Could I show you something else?" She held up the phone.

Todd's eyes widened in recognition. "That's her! That's definitely the woman he was bringing in. Always dressed nice."

Sammi felt a jolt of electricity run through her. "You're absolutely sure?"

"No doubt. That's James's 'assistant'." Todd made air quotes. "The one he was teaching to shoot."

"Beth Taylor," Sammi muttered, looking at the name on the profile.

"That fit with what I told your colleague? About how James acted with her?"

Sammi nodded, remembering Jake's notes. "It fits perfectly. He was more patient with her than with his wife. Stood closer than necessary."

"That's right." Todd nodded. "Wasn't hard to figure what was going on there."

"Thank you, Todd. This is extremely helpful." Sammi quickly took a screenshot of Beth's profile and tucked her phone away. As she pushed back through the glass door into the bitter cold, she couldn't help the smile spreading across her face.

Katherine would be pleased. Her first solo assignment, and she'd found something important. Something the others had missed. Not James's assistant Anna Bovill at all, but Beth Taylor, his mistress. Stamping her feet to keep warm, she checked the bus schedule. Ten minutes until the next one. Worth every second of the wait and the long ride back to the office. She tucked her scarf tighter around her neck, the cold no match for the warmth of her small victory.

The conservation lab felt like stepping into another world. Jake descended the concrete stairs to the basement level, following the signs to the east wing through a maze of utilitarian corridors that contrasted sharply with the museum's elegant public spaces above. The air grew cooler and carried the faint chemical odor of solvents and preservatives.

Behind a heavy door marked "Conservation Lab - Authorized Personnel Only," Jake found himself in a spacious room filled with specialized equipment. High-powered microscopes sat alongside infrared cameras, X-ray machines, and computers displaying magnified images of paint samples. Classical music played softly from hidden speakers.

Dr. Leonid Volkov stood hunched over a workbench, his silver hair tied back in a small ponytail. He wore a white lab coat over dark clothing and peered through a jeweler's loupe at what appeared to be a canvas fragment. He was a thin man, probably in his sixties, with the intense focus of someone accustomed to working alone.

"Dr. Volkov?" Jake called out, showing his badge as the scientist looked up with startled eyes.

"Yes? What is this about?" Volkov's accent carried traces of Eastern Europe, his voice cautious but not unfriendly.

"I'm private detective Jake Mercer. I'm investigating James Vanderlin's murder. I understand you worked with him recently on some authentication issues."

Volkov set down his loupe and straightened slowly, as if his back ached from long hours of hunching over his work. "Ah, poor James. Such a tragedy. Yes, we had many discussions about the Botticelli piece."

"The Harwicks mentioned you had several closed-door meetings with James before he died. What were you discussing?"

Volkov gestured to a pair of stools near his workstation and sighed. "Please, sit. James was ... how do I say diplomatically ... very thorough man. Sometimes too thorough." He removed his glasses and cleaned them. "The sketch is beautiful work and quite authentic, in my professional opinion. But James, he would not accept this."

"What do you mean?"

"Beth Taylor, she initially raised some questions about the piece. Probably just being cautious. It is an expensive acquisition, after all. But when I examined closely, everything looked authentic." Volkov walked to a computer terminal and pulled up high-resolution images. "The paper, the ink, the aging patterns, the style, all consistent with Botticelli workshop, fifteenth century."

Jake studied the magnified image on the screen. "So why did James keep pushing for more tests?"

"This is what I could never understand." Volkov shook his head. "I showed him results. Infrared spectroscopy, X-ray analysis, paper fiber dating. All supported authenticity. But James, he insisted on more and more testing. Even when Beth herself changed her mind and agreed piece was genuine, James would not let it go."

"That must have been frustrating."

"Very much so. I have other work to do, you understand? Important conservation projects that actually need my attention. But James kept scheduling meetings, asking for additional tests, questioning my methods." Volkov's tone held a note of professional irritation. "In forty years, I have rarely been so certain of a piece's authenticity. See? Every single test confirms what I told him from beginning."

"Did James seem worried about anything else? Did he mention feeling threatened?"

Volkov considered this. "Not threatened, no. But he was ... obsessed, I think is right word. Last time we spoke, three days before his death, I told him he needed to accept the evidence and move on. He said he couldn't let it go, that something felt wrong even if tests said otherwise."

"Did he give you any specifics about what felt wrong?"

"No, and this frustrated me greatly. In science, we rely on evidence, not feelings." Volkov gestured at his equipment. "These machines do not lie. But James, he seemed to think there was some conspiracy, some deception. I tried to reason with him, but ..." He shrugged helplessly.

Jake made notes. "In your opinion, was there any legitimate reason for James to continue questioning the Botticelli's authenticity?"

"None whatsoever." Volkov's response was firm. "The piece is genuine Renaissance work, properly acquired from reputable source in Florence. James's suspicions were unfounded, though I understand he meant well. Sometimes passion for artistic integrity can become ... how do you say ... unhealthy obsession."

The conservation scientist walked back to his workbench, his shoulders heavy with what seemed like regret. "I wish I could have convinced him to trust the science. Perhaps then he could have focused his energy on something more productive, and perhaps ..." He trailed off, not needing to finish the thought.

<h1 style="text-align:center">20</h1>

Katherine crouched beside the dangling wires where Camera Twelve should have been connected. The forensics team had already processed the area, but Katherine had learned long ago to trust her own observations.

"Amateur hour," she murmured, straightening up. "No attempt to hide the tampering. Just pulled the cables and walked away."

Lee clicked his tongue. "Too obvious. Like they wanted us to focus on this particular camera."

They were in the museum after hours—a small courtesy arranged by Frank Naylor after he learned about the "accident" with the falling crates. The empty halls amplified their footsteps as they moved through the service area.

"Camera Twelve covers what exactly?" Katherine asked, studying the layout on the security blueprints they had received from Kyle Bovill.

"The interior of the Baroque gallery, facing south." Lee's finger traced the path. "Where James's body was found."

Katherine nodded, mentally filing the information. "Show me what you found earlier."

Lee led her down the corridor to a small room filled with electrical panels and network equipment. A workspace had been improvised on a maintenance cart. Lee's laptop was connected to the security mainframe, multiple windows displaying camera feeds, blueprints, and code scrolling across the screen.

"This," Lee said with quiet admiration, "is a thing of beauty. Professionally speaking."

Katherine raised an eyebrow. "The security system?"

"The illusion of a security system." He tapped a few keys, bringing up a layout of the museum with colored cones representing camera coverage. "At first glance, it looks comprehensive. Every entrance, every gallery, every hallway appears to be covered."

"But?" Katherine prompted, reading his expression.

"But someone knew exactly what they were doing." Lee hit another key, and red lines appeared on the blueprint. "There's a path. Service entrance to Baroque gallery, avoiding every camera. Not by luck. By design."

Katherine leaned closer, studying the red path that wound through service corridors, storage rooms, and staff hallways. "That's not possible without insider knowledge of the camera placements. Kyle Bovill designed the system."

"Right, and if it had been installed according to these blueprints," Lee shook the printed papers in his hand, "it would work perfectly. But it wasn't."

"Someone didn't install all of the cameras?"

Lee grinned. "No, much more sophisticated than that." He pulled up another building schematic on his computer with several cameras highlighted. "These six cameras," he pointed them out on the blueprint, "were installed in the correct locations. But critically, not at the correct angle."

"A careless mistake?"

"No way. This level of precision suggests whoever installed the system intentionally created these blind spots."

"Gavin Tucker." Katherine recalled the name of the technician who installed the system.

"The very same." Lee nodded. "The system was a gift from James Vanderlin to the museum. It was a surprise for his wife."

Katherine straightened, thinking about the video footage. "I wonder if Misty knew about the new security system."

Lee shook his head. "I don't think it would have mattered. The cameras are more or less in the same place as they were before. The one or two 'new' locations were nowhere near the Baroque exhibit. The main difference between this system and the old one is that it is all digital. No more VHS tapes. And the cameras have some automatic adjustment features for low light conditions."

"So someone modified Kyle Bovill's security system to create a backdoor into the museum, hidden from sight."

"And someone followed this secret path and put a bullet in James Vanderlin," Lee finished.

Katherine's phone vibrated in her pocket. "Hi, Sammi," she answered, putting the call on speaker.

"Katherine!" Sammi's voice crackled with excitement. "I found something huge. Remember how Jake visited that gun club where James took his 'assistant' for shooting lessons?"

"Yes?..."

"Well, I just confirmed with the manager," Sammi rushed on. "Guess who the 'assistant' was? Beth Taylor! The same Beth who found the body, who's pregnant with James's baby, and who just got promoted to interim curator!"

Katherine felt her pulse quicken. "Are you certain?"

"Hundred percent," Sammi confirmed. "Todd is positive that Beth is the woman who was coming in with James. And get this, she was practicing with a Glock 19."

"The same model as Misty's gun," Katherine noted, exchanging glances with Lee.

"Exactly! And I was thinking about something that Agent Chen said, 'Pillow talk happens.' If the FBI thinks that James might have leaked information to his wife, why couldn't he have leaked the information to his lover?"

"Sammi, good work." Katherine said. "Check if Beth Taylor has any connection to foreign entities or competitors of Meridian Tech."

"Already on it," Sammi replied.

After ending the call, Katherine dialed Beth Taylor's number.

The phone rang twice before Beth's voice came through, artificially bright.

"Detective Carson! What a surprise. How can I help you?"

Katherine didn't bother with pleasantries. "Do you know how to shoot a gun?"

The silence stretched so long, Katherine wondered if the call had dropped. When Beth finally spoke, her voice had changed— flatter, more careful.

"Why would you ask me that?"

"Just answer the question."

Another pause. Then Beth let out a long sigh that sounded almost theatrical. "Yes, I know how to shoot. James taught me. He said a woman should know how to protect herself."

"Why didn't you tell anyone this before?"

Beth's laugh was sharp and bitter. "Oh, come on. For obvious reasons, right? James is dead, shot with a gun, and here I am—the other woman—who just happens to know how to use a firearm. How do you think that looks?"

"It doesn't look good, Beth."

"Look, I know what you're thinking, but you're barking up the wrong tree. Misty killed him. I'm sure of it. That woman was consumed with jealousy, and she had access to James's gun. She knew he was leaving her."

"How can you be so certain—"

"Because I know things," Beth interrupted. "Things about that marriage. Things about what Misty was capable of." She paused, and when she continued, there was something calculating in her voice. "You know what? You might as well hear all of it. Come over to my house tomorrow morning. Nine o'clock sharp. Don't be late."

The line went dead.

Katherine stared at the phone in her hand. "That was strange." She relayed the conversation to Lee, who was running a few more diagnostics on the security system.

Lee raised an eyebrow. "Are you going to meet her?"

"I don't think I have a choice." Katherine sighed. "Beth knows a lot more than she is saying about this murder."

"Want me to come with you? In case you're walking into another trap?"

"That's a good idea. In the meantime, let's test your theory." She gestured to the door. "Show me this invisible path through the museum."

For the next hour, they moved methodically through the museum, following the path Lee had identified. Katherine noted how each turn and corridor seemed innocuous on its own, but together they created a perfectly concealed route to the Baroque gallery.

"This is professional work," she said as they paused in a storage area. "Intelligence community level."

Lee nodded. "The kind of thing we'd set up for asset extraction. You thinking black ops?"

"I'm thinking someone with training," Katherine replied. "The level of marksmanship Rhonda mentioned combined with this security setup? This wasn't just a jealous lover."

They reached the end of the path, a small service door that opened directly into the northeast corner of the Baroque gallery, exactly where James's body had been found.

"Not even a squeak," Katherine said as Lee gently pushed the door open. "Well-maintained hinges."

"Of course," Lee agreed. "Can't have noise giving away your position."

They stepped into the gallery, now restored to its normal state, the crime scene tape removed. Katherine moved to the exact spot where James had fallen, mentally calculating angles and distances.

"From here," she said, "someone entering through that service door would have a clear shot without being visible from the main entrance."

Lee nodded. "And Camera Twelve—the one that was disabled—would have been the only one to catch someone using this path."

"Too perfect to be coincidental," Katherine concluded, turning slowly to take in the entire gallery. "Misty walked into a trap the moment she entered this gallery."

Lee nodded grimly. "The security camera blackout, the murder weapon, the location. It was a perfect setup."

✌

Jake caught up with Security Chief Frank Naylor as the man was gathering his coat and keys.

"Mr. Naylor?" Jake reached into his jacket and produced his credentials. "I'm Jake Mercer, with Carson Investigations. Just need a quick word about the Vanderlin case."

"Of course. Though I was hoping to get home to dinner with the family."

"I won't take much of your time." Jake glanced at the bank of monitors showing the security feeds. "I understand you've been upgrading your security system this week."

"That's right. Been a phased installation all week," Naylor said.

"When exactly did you lose video coverage in the offices?"

"Let's see ..." Naylor flipped open a file folder on his desk. "Old cameras in the administrative wing came out Thursday evening. New cameras weren't installed until Friday afternoon."

Jake sensed a connection forming. "So Friday morning, the administrative areas had no surveillance at all."

"Unfortunately, yes. Maybe a four-hour window after the museum opened."

"What about Misty Vanderlin's office specifically? Could someone have accessed it Friday morning?"

Naylor shifted uncomfortably. "Yes. Anyone with badge access could have entered undetected."

Jake made a note. "Before the murder that night."

"Theoretically." Naylor's military bearing couldn't quite hide his discomfort with the security breach.

"Her phone, for instance. If she'd left it in her office, someone could have entered and used her phone without anyone the wiser."

Naylor nodded reluctantly. "I suppose that's possible."

"Who has administrative wing access?"

"All senior staff. Curators, department heads, myself." He paused. "Board members with special clearance."

"Can you pull badge swipes for Friday morning? Say, eight AM to noon?"

"Badge system's on a separate network. Still functional." Naylor moved to his computer. "Give me a minute."

The printer whirred briefly. Jake scanned the short list of entries, noting the expected pattern of office access during normal work hours.

"Looks like administrative staff accessing their own offices." Jake paused at one entry. "Plus Misty herself at 8:15 AM. And this one—guest badge G-447, multiple entries between 8:30 AM and 11:45 AM."

Naylor cross-referenced the guest badge number. "That's Gavin Tucker. The security technician installing the cameras."

"He was working in the administrative wing all morning?"

"That's right. I was overseeing the gallery installations."

Jake felt the pieces aligning. "So Tucker had unsupervised access to every office in the wing, including Misty's."

"For about two hours, yes." Naylor's expression shifted as the implications hit him. "You think Tucker took the phone?"

"I think a security technician with unrestricted access and no oversight had the perfect opportunity." Jake folded the paper. "Question is whether he was acting on his own initiative or someone else's instructions."

As Naylor locked his office, Jake headed for the exit. Gavin Tucker had unsupervised access to Misty's office during the surveillance gap. Now he needed to track down the security technician and find out what else he might have done while installing those cameras.

21

Katherine adjusted her position in the driver's seat, eyes fixed on the nondescript office building across the street. Christopher Euler had been inside for forty-three minutes. Long enough for more than a routine meeting.

Her phone buzzed. Jake's voice came through the earpiece. "Package delivery coming your way."

She glanced in the rearview mirror, watching him approach with his measured stride. He slipped into the passenger seat, setting a white and blue paper bag between them.

"Attman's!" Katherine smiled.

"Pastrami and Swiss from your favorite deli."

"Thanks." She unwrapped the sandwich but kept her focus on the building's entrance. "Euler's still inside. Third floor, corner office. Blinds closed."

Jake followed her gaze. "Any movement?"

"Two men went up about twenty minutes after he arrived. Designer suits, briefcases." Katherine took a bite, chewing thoughtfully. "Cash transaction, if I had to guess."

"When are you going to tell our client what you've found? And the police?"

"When I have solid proof." Katherine took another bite and chewed slowly, savoring the mixture of coriander and caraway. "It'll be my word against his at the moment."

They ate in comfortable silence. The distant sound of sirens echoed from somewhere in the city.

Movement in the third-floor window caught Katherine's attention. The blinds had shifted slightly.

"Activity," she murmured, raising the camera.

Jake leaned forward, scanning the building's entrances. "Could be them wrapping up."

"Or bringing in more participants." Katherine adjusted the camera focus. "This is bigger than simple fraud. This is organized crime territory."

"Which means Euler's either in deep or he's about to be."

"My gut says he's been in deep for a while. The question is whether he knows how deep."

They fell into focused silence, both of them shifting into full surveillance mode. But Katherine found herself thinking about her conversation with Dr. Reed and the suggestion that hyper-vigilance might be costing her something essential.

"I saw Dr. Emily Reed today," she said quietly.

"How did it go?" Jake asked.

"Better than I expected." Katherine shifted in her seat, turning more towards him. "She gets it. The work, I mean. She didn't need me to explain operational protocols or why I carry the knife everywhere."

"That's the advantage of Agency-cleared therapists." Jake smiled. "What did you talk about?"

"She asked if I ever feel like I'm watching someone else live my life."

"And?"

"I told her the truth. Some days, it's like I'm going through the motions. Other days, the grief hits like shrapnel—sudden, sharp, unexpected."

A car pulled up across the street, but it was just someone visiting the building next door. Katherine tracked its movement before returning her attention to Euler's location.

"We talked about anger," she said after a moment. "At my former superiors. At the situation." Her voice got quieter. "At Daniel for leaving me. Then the guilt that follows the anger."

"Same cycle you've been in since the funeral."

Katherine nodded. She didn't need to explain to Jake. The grief, the guilt, the anger, the compartmentalization ... he'd seen it all. The self-doubt was the worst part. Without Daniel's steadying presence, she found herself questioning every decision, every instinct that once felt certain. Without Jake's support, Katherine didn't know where she'd be.

She checked her watch again. "Emily wants to see me again next week. Said the first session was just establishing a baseline. The real work starts with session two."

"How do you feel about that?"

Katherine was quiet for a moment, watching the building across the street. "Nervous. But not resistant. That's progress, I think."

"Definitely progress."

"Two men approaching the building," Katherine's profess-sional focus snapped back into place. "Same type as before."

Jake leaned forward, observing. "Different car this time. They're rotating vehicles."

"Smart. Suggests they're concerned about surveillance." Katherine reached for her camera, adjusting the telephoto lens. "Or they're just cautious by nature."

"My money's on the former. This feels too organized for casual business."

They watched as the men entered the building, their movements efficient and purposeful.

"Euler's running a regular operation here," Katherine observed. "Multiple meetings, rotating contacts. It's structured."

After a few minutes of silence, Jake asked, "So, did Dr. Reed give you some good insight?"

"Yeah. She also said healing doesn't mean forgetting Daniel. It means integrating his influence into who I'm becoming."

"That sounds right." Jake's voice carried a note of relief.

Katherine remembered the countless times over the years that he had said something similar. She nodded. "Emily asked me to pay attention to moments when I feel genuinely engaged. Not just functioning, but actually present. Even if that means letting myself feel the grief and all the emotions that come with it." She was quiet for a moment, watching a pedestrian cross the street below Euler's building. "She suggested it might help to get back to teaching."

Jake raised an eyebrow. "Agency classes?"

"No. Maybe something like Margaret does with the criminology department at the University of Baltimore, or ..." Katherine was quiet for a moment, tapping the steering wheel. "She knows about the art history degree."

Jake broke into a smile. "Art appreciation classes?"

"Maybe. There's something appealing about sharing knowledge that doesn't involve weapons or surveillance techniques." Katherine's love of art was something they'd discovered together when she was twelve and he'd taken her to the Walters Art Museum for the first time. She'd stood transfixed in front of a Monet for twenty minutes.

Jake's tone was warm. "That's a great idea, Katie. You deserve to do something you love for a change. You always could make those museum visits come alive when you'd drag me along."

"The art thing is complicated," Katherine admitted. "Daniel and I used to spend weekends at galleries. The Met when we were in New York, the National Gallery in D.C.. It was our refuge from the work."

"And now it hurts too much?"

"Yes." Katherine's voice cracked. "But maybe it's the one thing I should be protecting."

"What would Daniel want for you?" Jake asked softly.

Katherine was quiet for a long moment. When she spoke, her voice was barely above a whisper. "To stop punishing myself for surviving. To find something beyond just getting through each day."

The two men from earlier emerged from the building, moving quickly toward a different car than the one they'd arrived in.

"Target rotation," Katherine said, professional mask sliding back into place.

"Same drill as before?"

"Likely. Euler will wait fifteen minutes, then exit through the rear." She started the engine but didn't put the car in gear yet. "Standard protocol for avoiding association."

As they watched the men drive away, Katherine felt something shift inside her—not the weight disappearing, but perhaps, for the first time in years, the recognition that it might not have to define everything she chose to do next.

"Ready?"

Katherine checked her mirrors, confirmed their target was still in the building, and nodded. "Let's see where Christopher Euler goes when he thinks nobody's watching."

Movement in the building's rear exit caught their attention. Christopher Euler emerged, hurrying toward a silver Buick.

"Target's mobile," Katherine announced. She eased the car into traffic, maintaining a careful three-car distance behind Euler's silver Buick.

"He's heading east," Jake observed, checking the side mirror. "Away from his office, away from his apartment."

"Third location," Katherine murmured, her fingers drumming against the steering wheel. "Classic laundering protocol. Never conduct business where you live or work."

The Buick signaled right onto Eastern Avenue. Katherine waited for a delivery truck to pass before following.

"What's down this way?" Jake asked, studying the neighborhood. Industrial buildings gave way to a mix of warehouses and small businesses, the kind of area where cash transactions wouldn't raise eyebrows.

"Port access. Shipping containers, freight companies." Katherine recognized the area. "Perfect for moving more than just money."

Euler's brake lights flashed as he turned into the parking lot of a small freight company called Maritime Solutions. The building's faded blue paint and minimal signage suggested the business preferred anonymity.

Katherine drove past the entrance, parking half a block down where they could observe through the chain-link fence. She killed the engine and reached for her camera.

"Two other cars already here," Jake noted, his experienced eye cataloging details. "Black Mercedes, white Escalade. Both with tinted windows."

"High-end vehicles for a freight company." Katherine adjusted the telephoto lens, focusing on Euler as he approached the building's side entrance. "Someone's doing very well in the shipping business."

Through the viewfinder, she watched Euler approach the door. The door opened before he reached it, as if someone had been waiting.

"Expected guest," she said, clicking photos. "This isn't his first visit."

Jake studied the building through binoculars. "Security cameras on all corners, but they're angled to watch the perimeter, not document who comes and goes. Someone knows how to avoid creating evidence."

A man emerged from the building, his athletic build apparent despite the heavy coat he wore. His breath formed clouds in the frigid air as he lit a cigarette and began scanning the parking lot.

"Muscle." Katherine clicked the shutter. "Professional grade."

"Look at his military stance." Jake lowered his binoculars. "This guy's not just hired security."

The man's methodical scan of the area made Katherine slide lower in her seat. His gaze swept past their position once, then returned, lingering on their car for several seconds. His casual demeanor sharpened into alert focus.

"We're made," she whispered, setting the camera in her lap.

The man took a long drag of his cigarette, never taking his eyes off their position. Then he flicked the cigarette into the snow and reached into his coat.

"Time to go," Jake whispered.

Katherine didn't need to be told twice. She started the engine. Through her peripheral vision, she saw the man pull out a phone.

"He's calling it in," she said, pulling away from the curb. "Whatever they're doing in there, they take security seriously."

22

Katherine leaned against a cement block wall, her arms crossed tightly over her chest. She had kept quiet so far, not wanting to get involved in the awkward conversation happening between her friend Margaret and their client, Misty Vanderlin. But watching Misty's anguish stirred something familiar and painful in her chest. The raw confusion of losing not just a husband, but the version of yourself that existed alongside him.

"I can't believe you didn't tell me, Misty. Not as your lawyer, not as your friend. You let me walk into this blind." Margaret was pacing, her eyes blazing with a mixture of hurt and disbelief.

"I didn't want you to think badly of him." Misty's voice was small, almost ashamed. Her hands were twisting together in her lap. "I didn't want to think badly of him myself. If I didn't say it out loud, maybe it wasn't real."

Margaret's hand went to her forehead, rubbing in slow, deliberate motions. "But you knew."

Misty swallowed, shaking her head as if trying to deny the truth even now. "I didn't believe it. Not really. I couldn't. Because if James wasn't who I thought he was, then who was I? The woman who loved a faithful husband, or the fool married to a cheater?"

"When did you find out?" Margaret asked, some of the fire leaving.

Misty closed her eyes. "Kyle Bovill approached me at their Halloween party a few months ago. He told me about James and Beth and said I could get back at James by ... by having an affair with him."

Margaret's face paled. "And you didn't believe him?" she asked, her voice taut.

"I didn't want to believe," Misty whispered, her shoulders slumping. "Because believing Kyle meant everything I thought I knew about my marriage was a lie. Everything I thought I knew about myself."

"What else aren't you telling me? Did you do it?" Margaret's expression grew darker. "Did you have an affair? Did you kill James to keep him from finding out?"

Misty's eyes welled up with tears, her lips trembling. "I didn't do it. I swear, Margaret, I didn't have an affair. And I didn't kill James." Her voice cracked, her face turning pale with panic. "I didn't want this. I never wanted this." She wiped her eyes hastily.

Margaret looked at Katherine and then back to Misty, torn between her hope and her suspicions.

Katherine took a deep breath, thinking about her conversation with Dr. Reed yesterday. She stepped forward, her voice steady and firm. "Misty, I know how it feels to be a widow. I also know how it feels to lose a version of yourself."

Misty's face crumpled, her whole body shaking with the force of her sobs. "I don't know who I am anymore," she whispered. "I was James's wife. I was the woman married to the man who brought me flowers every Friday and called me beautiful every morning. Now I don't know if any of that was real."

Katherine moved closer, her own eyes glistening. "It was real, Misty. Your love was real. Your grief is real." She paused, letting her own emotions wash over her. For the first time in eight years, she didn't push them away.

"How do you do it?" Misty asked, her voice breaking. "How do you figure out who you are when everything you thought you knew turns out to be wrong?"

"One day at a time," Katherine said softly. She echoed some of the words her new therapist had said to her. "You grieve. Not just for James, but for the version of your life you thought you had. You get help. You learn that the mistakes others made, the mistakes you've made, don't define your worth."

Katherine's voice remained gentle. "James supported your career at the museum. Was the financial pressure difficult? I imagine funding is always tight for arts institutions."

Misty's hands stilled in her lap. "The museum is fine. James's support was ... emotional, not financial." She looked to Margaret. "I just need to figure out who I am without him."

Margaret wrapped her arms around Misty, the two of them crying together. Margaret looked at Katherine and mouthed, "Thank you."

Katherine smiled, although tears still filled her eyes. She wasn't used to being this open and vulnerable with virtual strangers. But maybe this was how healing was supposed to feel.

Misty wiped her eyes, something shifting in her posture. "I can't explain what happened that night. All I know is that James was alive when I stepped out of the room. When I came back, he was laying there in the middle of the floor."

"Didn't you hear the gunshot?" Margaret asked.

Misty shook her head.

"In the middle of the floor?" Katherine repeated, wiping her own eyes as her investigative instincts took over again. "What else did you see?"

Misty blew her nose. "James on the floor, and a pool of blood. I didn't hear anything."

"Where was the blood?" Katherine asked, forgetting to be delicate. Something was tickling the back of her mind.

"Next to his head. Next to the gun." Misty's voice shook. "My gun."

Katherine looked at Margaret. "But you never took your gun out of the safe?"

"No! Never. James must have taken it."

"Did you see the wound?" Katherine questioned.

"What?"

"The bullet wound. Where your husband was shot. Did you see it?"

Misty trembled. "No, I just saw the blood, and James, and the gun. I was in a room with restricted access and I knew everything would point to me. So I just ran."

Katherine's gaze softened and a smile crept across her face. Not just because Misty was finally telling the truth, but because now she had an idea how someone could have framed her in such a small window of time.

Lee was already at his desk when Sammi burst through the office door, her laptop bag slung over her shoulder.

"Buenos días, Lee!" she called out, dropping her bag with a thud. "You're here early. Did you even go home last night?"

Lee looked up from his computer screen, rubbing his eyes. "Barely. Katherine and I were at the museum until almost midnight." He gestured to the security blueprints spread across his desk. "Found some interesting things, though."

Sammi pulled up a chair, her dark eyes bright with curiosity. "Oh? What did you find?"

"Well," Lee leaned back in his chair, "turns out the new security system was sabotaged. Professionally."

"Sabotaged how?"

Lee pointed out the marked areas on the blueprints. "Six cameras were installed at the wrong angles. Not by accident— by design. Created a perfect invisible path from the service entrance straight to where James was killed."

Sammi stared at the blueprints. "Who do you think is responsible?"

"As far as we know, Gavin Tucker is the only person who had access to the cameras. He was responsible for installing the new system."

Sammi wrinkled her brow, examining the blueprints and Lee's notes. "Gavin is about my age, right?"

"Yeah. Someone your age could set this up, couldn't they?"

"Sure, if they knew what they were doing. But why would they? I mean, seriously. Why go to all this trouble when you could just cut all the cameras? Anyone with basic tech knowledge could disable a security system."

Lee raised an eyebrow. "Go on."

"Think about it!" Sammi stood up, pacing behind her chair. "We're working under the assumption that someone is trying to frame Misty, right? But this setup is so … elaborate. I know you guys have way more experience with spy craft than I do, but does Gavin Tucker strike you as someone with intelligence training?"

"Not particularly," Lee admitted.

"Exactly! So why would he risk positioning cameras with blind spots when he could just cut the whole system?" Sammi's voice picked up speed, the way it always did when her mind was racing. "Even without the other camera footage, the frame would still be pretty damning! You'd still have footage of Misty letting James into the museum after hours, leading him to the murder room. Then cut all the cameras, and her fingerprints are on the gun—her gun. That's still a solid case, even without the camera footage showing the actual murder."

Lee leaned forward, intrigued. "So why the elaborate extra steps?"

"This seems so intentional about framing Misty." Sammi stopped pacing. "They could have killed James anywhere else—in the parking lot, at his office, at home. They could have cut the power and killed him in the museum and just let the chips fall where they may. But no, they wanted Misty to be the one blamed, and they wanted the case against her to be airtight."

Lee stared at the blueprint for a long moment. "You know what? Your gut's telling you Gavin didn't do this."

"My gut's screaming it," Sammi said firmly. "Even if someone paid him to adjust the camera angles, he'd be taking a huge risk. The tampering would point straight back to him as the main suspect."

"This level of planning, this specific targeting of Misty... someone *really* wanted her to go down for this murder. The question is who, and why?"

23

Jake knelt beside the Vanderlins' bedroom safe, photographing the empty outline in the dark velvet where Misty's Glock 19 should have been. No scratches on the exterior of the safe, no damage to the locking mechanism. No forced entry. Whoever removed the gun had the combination to the safe.

Jake checked his watch and headed for his Jeep. Time to see if James's office safe told the same story.

Owen Lacroix looked older than during their first interview. He unlocked James's office with shaking hands. "The feds have been through everything twice."

"I need to see James's gun safe," Jake said.

Lacroix moved to the bookshelf, sliding aside a leather-bound volume to reveal a keypad. His fingers hesitated. "I probably shouldn't—"

"We're trying to understand how the murder weapon was accessed. Misty's life is on the line."

The safe clicked open. Like the bedroom safe, it held documents and cash. And like the bedroom safe, it contained an empty foam outline where a Glock 19 should have been.

"James's gun is gone too," Jake observed.

Lacroix went pale. "That's impossible. No one else has the combination."

"No one?"

"Well, I have it for emergencies. And..." Lacroix hesitated. "Anna might have seen James enter it."

"You think Anna memorized the combination?"

"Anna pays attention to everything. She probably knew James's routines better than his wife did." Lacroix sank into a chair. "Dear God, you think Anna took both guns?"

Jake examined the locking mechanism. No damage, no tampering. Professional work. "Someone with authorized access removed both weapons from secure locations. That's not random crime, Mr. Lacroix. That's an inside job. We need to report this immediately," Jake said. "Both weapons are in the wind."

Jake texted Katherine: "Both guns missing from safes. Be careful."

Katherine's response came immediately: "I know where the second gun is."

⁂

Katherine pulled into the parking space outside Beth Taylor's apartment building at exactly 8:57 AM.

"You sure about this?" Lee asked from the passenger seat, adjusting his jacket against the morning chill. "Woman sounded a little unhinged on that phone call."

"That's exactly why we need to hear what she has to say." Katherine stepped out of the car, her breath visible in the cold air. "Beth knows more than she's letting on. The way she deflected, then suddenly wanted to talk, that's not random."

They climbed the stairs to the second floor. Apartment 4B sat at the end of the hallway, its dark wooden door looking ordinary enough. She knocked firmly, three measured raps.

Silence.

"Beth? It's Katherine Carson. We had an appointment."

Lee slouched against the wall behind her. "Maybe she changed her mind. Got spooked."

Katherine knocked again, harder this time. "Beth Taylor, we're here to talk like you asked."

Still nothing. She pressed her ear to the door, listening for movement inside. No footsteps, no television, no signs of life at all.

She pulled out her phone and dialed Beth's number. From inside the apartment, they could hear Beth's phone ring. No answer.

"This doesn't feel right," Katherine said.

Lee nodded, standing up straighter as Katherine reached for the door handle. It turned easily and the door opened with a soft creak.

"Beth?" she called out. "We're coming in."

The familiar fragrance of vanilla and old wood hit her just as she remembered from their previous visit. But underneath it, another smell. Something metallic and wrong.

Lee drew his Glock, and Katherine let him take point as they moved into the apartment. The living room looked exactly as it had before: cream walls adorned with Klimt and Monet reproductions, the sleek gray couch positioned across from the armchair where Beth had sat so gracefully.

Except now Beth was on the floor behind that chair.

"Damn," Lee breathed, lowering his weapon.

"Clear the other rooms," Katherine ordered as she crouched to get a closer look at the body crumpled on the hardwood floor.

It was clear that Beth Taylor was already dead. A single gunshot wound to the head. Blood had pooled beneath her, staining the light wood.

Katherine dialed 911. "This is Katherine Carson, private detective. I need police and CSI at 101 West Read Street, Apartment 4B. We have a homicide."

While she relayed the details, Lee finished sweeping the apartment. "All clear," he said, holstering his weapon. "What've we got?"

"Single shot, in the back of the head. Close range," Katherine observed. "And look at this." She pointed to a gun lying about three feet from Beth's outstretched hand—a custom Glock 19 that looked oddly familiar.

Lee whistled low. "That the same weapon from the Vanderlin scene?"

"Looks like it. We'll need ballistics to confirm, but ..." Katherine studied the positioning. "This is sloppy work. Whoever did this was either in a hurry or not as careful as they were at the museum."

She stood, pulling out her phone. "The Vanderlin murder was clean, professional. Minimal blood spatter, weapon placement that suggested staging. This?" She gestured around the room. "This looks like panic."

Lee was examining the apartment's entry points. "No signs of forced entry. She either knew her killer or they had a key."

"Look at her hands." Katherine pointed out Beth's manicured fingers. No defensive wounds, no signs of a struggle. Her clothing was neat, undisturbed.

"She knew whoever did this," Katherine concluded. "Trusted them enough to turn her back."

"Or they surprised her. But given the trajectory," Lee crouched, studying the angle, "she was standing when she was shot. Probably facing away from the shooter."

"What bothers me most is the timing. Yesterday, Beth seemed anxious to talk. Said she knows things about Misty and James that could blow this case open. Twelve hours later, she's dead." Katherine moved toward the window, careful not to disturb potential evidence. "Either this is the worst coincidence in investigative history, or someone was listening to our phone call."

Lee's expression darkened. "You thinking our communications are compromised?"

"I'm thinking Beth Taylor knew something that got her killed. And whoever did this wanted to make sure she never got the chance to tell us what it was."

The sound of sirens grew louder outside. Katherine stared down at Beth's body, remembering the woman's artificial brightness on the phone, the way her voice had changed when Katherine asked about guns. The calculated tone when she'd insisted Misty was the killer.

"You were wrong about one thing, Beth," Katherine murmured. "You said Misty killed James. But Misty's still in lockup. Which means whoever really killed your lover just made sure you'd never point us in the right direction."

24

Jake pushed through the office door. "Afternoon, Sammi." He settled into one of the couches without removing his jacket. "Katherine still out?"

"Yeah, but she should be back any minute." Sammi looked up from her computer screen, fingers still poised over the keyboard. "You find anything useful at the museum last night?"

Jake nodded, his expression serious. "Confirmed what we suspected. Someone could definitely access Misty's office during the timeframe when that text was sent. And Gavin Tucker's guest badge was used to enter the administrative wing multiple times during the period when the cameras were disabled."

Sammi's eyes widened. "So he was definitely there." She crossed her arms. "I've tried to call like six times already. It's going straight to voicemail."

"What about those phone records the police shared?"

"Now, that's interesting." Sammi typed enthusiastically at her computer. "Come here," she said, waving him over. "The text from Misty's phone was sent during lunch hour—12:47 PM to be exact. But here's the thing, it was deleted from her phone immediately after."

Jake's brow furrowed as he looked over her shoulder. "Deleted how?"

"Someone went into her text messages and manually deleted the conversation thread." Sammi opened her phone's text message app to demonstrate. "But see, when you delete a text from your phone, it doesn't just disappear completely. The phone companies keep records of all message traffic on their networks."

"So the police can still see it."

"Exactly! The carrier can find the sender, receiver, timestamp, even the content if it's not encrypted. It's like ... imagine if every letter you sent was photocopied by the post office before delivery."

Jake thought through the meaning behind this information. "The police report only shows that Misty's phone sent the message."

"Right." Sammi's expression grew more serious. "They know the phone sent it, but they have no way to prove that Misty actually typed the message. Anyone who had access to her phone during that time could have sent it."

"And then deleted it to cover their tracks." Jake's voice carried the grim recognition of someone who understood operational security. "Smart move, if you're thinking the phone won't be examined closely."

"But not smart enough," Sammi said with satisfaction. "Because they didn't count on the police pulling the carrier records. Most people don't realize how much digital evidence exists even after you think you've erased it."

Jake stood, checking his watch. "So we've got Gavin's badge accessing the administrative wing, someone with physical access to Misty's phone, and a deleted message that makes Misty look guilty."

"And Gavin Tucker, who suddenly doesn't want to take phone calls." Sammi saved her work.

"When Katherine gets back," Jake said, moving to the window, "we are headed to D.C. I'm going to track down Gavin Tucker once and for all. And Kat's got an important meeting with the FBI."

"Cool!" Sammi grinned. "What's she going to do at the FBI?"

"Hopefully she's going to get us something useful about their investigation into Meridian Tech." *And hopefully,* he thought, *she'll start to reconnect to her purpose.*

ॐ

The Jeep's heater fought against the January cold as Jake merged onto I-95 North. Katherine stared out the passenger window at the gray Baltimore skyline giving way to suburban sprawl, her hands clasped tightly in her lap.

"You don't have to do this if you're not ready." Jake glanced at her profile. "I can handle the FBI meeting."

Katherine shook her head. "I need to do this. Gregory Irvine owes me more than one favor, and Agent Chen wasn't exactly forthcoming with you." She paused, then added quietly, "Besides, I can't keep running from every difficult conversation."

Jake nodded, understanding the weight behind her words. They drove in silence for several miles before she spoke again.

"I should have seen it coming. Beth's murder."

"Katie—"

"No, hear me out." Her voice was steady, controlled. "At first she didn't want to talk. She was dismissive of my questions." She turned toward Jake. "Then her whole tone changed mid-conversation. Almost like she was taunting someone."

Jake kept his eyes on the road. "You think someone was there with her?"

"Had to be. The rigor mortis was already set when we found her. She must have been killed shortly after we spoke."

"The gun?"

"Registered to James Vanderlin. One of a pair. But the scene was sloppy and rushed. No careful staging like the museum." She exhaled slowly. "Whoever killed James took time to frame Misty perfectly." Katherine rubbed her temples. "Beth knew something that scared someone enough to risk exposure."

Jake looked at Katherine as traffic slowed to a crawl. "Speaking of exposure, I got a name from our Maritime Solutions contact."

Katherine straightened. "The suit Euler met with?"

"Quinn Pham. Runs a legitimate freight operation on the surface, but my source says he's been running high-end smuggling operations for years." Jake grimaced. "The kind where investors put up cash for shipments of art, antiquities, other valuable items that move through ports with minimal scrutiny."

Katherine processed this as they took the exit for Washington. "So we have one case involving money laundering that leads to an art smuggler. And a murder investigation where the victims were involved with investigating art fraud, getting paranoid about conspiracies."

"Could be coincidence. Art's a high-value target for both legitimate fraud and black-market operations." Jake paused, considering. "But two separate art-related cases surfacing at the same time..." He glanced at Katherine. "We can't force connections that aren't there, but we can't ignore the pattern either."

"Greg might have intel on whether Pham's operation intersects with museum or gallery networks."

"Right," Jake agreed. "Gregory Irvine has access to databases Chen can't or won't share."

Katherine nodded, then looked at Jake. "Thank you. For understanding why I need to do this myself."

"Katie, after everything we've been through together—" Jake's voice softened. "You don't have to prove anything to me. But if this helps you find your footing again, then I'm all for it."

FBI Headquarters loomed ahead. Katherine checked her watch. They'd made good time despite the traffic.

"Find Gavin," she said as she exited the Jeep. "Whatever happened at the museum that night, that kid is in the middle of it."

"Understood."

"And Jake?" Katherine paused as she closed the door. "Thanks."

25

The J. Edgar Hoover Building felt exactly as Katherine remembered. Sterile corridors lined with portraits of former directors and the unique smell of government coffee and ambition. She'd been here countless times during her ESA years, back when the lines between agencies blurred in the shadows of mutually assured destruction.

Katherine adjusted her jacket as she approached the elevator bank. Eight years of civilian life hadn't dulled her instincts. The building's rhythms came back to her: the way guards positioned themselves, the subtle camera angles, the coded conversations that drifted through the halls.

"Katherine Carson." The receptionist's voice carried a note of recognition that meant her clearance was still active. Good. Some strings still held.

Deputy Assistant Director Gregory Irvine's office overlooked Pennsylvania Avenue, a corner suite that spoke to two decades of careful career navigation. Irvine stood as she entered, his smile genuine despite the circumstances.

"Kat. You look good." He gestured to the leather chairs arranged in one corner of the room. "Civilian life agrees with you."

"Most days." Katherine settled into the chair, noting how Irvine positioned himself angled toward the door, back to the wall. Old habits. "Thanks for seeing me, Greg."

"When Katherine Carson calls in a favor, I listen. Though I have to say, Agent Chen is less than thrilled about this meeting."

They chatted comfortably for nearly a half hour. Greg caught her up on some of the latest agency gossip, and Katherine gave her civilian perspective on a few cases. Finally, Agent Chen appeared in the doorway. His jaw was set, shoulders rigid with barely contained irritation.

"Agent Chen." Katherine didn't stand. "Enjoying your coffee shop meetings?"

Chen's eyes flashed. "Ms. Carson. I wasn't aware private detectives held security clearances sufficient for this level of briefing."

"They don't." Katherine kept her voice level, even though Chen's tone rubbed her the wrong way. "But former ESA operatives do."

Irvine cleared his throat and gestured for Chen to sit.

"Chen, Katherine spent seventeen years with the Espionage Services Agency. Her clearance remains active per standard protocol." Irvine's tone carried the weight of bureaucratic finality. "She's here in an official consultative capacity."

Chen sat, but his posture remained defensive. "Sir, with respect, this investigation involves sensitive national security matters. A private detective—"

"Who used to run HUMINT operations in Eastern Europe," Katherine interjected. "Who still has contacts in fourteen countries and knows exactly how intelligence flows through corporate channels." She leaned forward, gaining confidence. "Agent Chen, I was running covert operations while you were still asking your college professors what FARA stood for. My clearance predates your career by about a decade." She settled back in her chair. "But thanks for the security lesson."

Irvine nodded. "Brief her, Chen. Full disclosure."

Chen's jaw worked silently before he spoke. "Meridian Tech has been under investigation for eighteen months. Suspected intellectual property theft, specifically quantum encryption algorithms, developed under defense contracts."

"CFIUS review triggered the investigation?" Katherine asked.

"Initially. But the scope expanded when we identified unusual financial patterns." Chen opened a file, flipping through documents. "James Vanderlin, as Meridian's CFO, had access to compartmentalized financial data. Wire transfers to shell companies, consultancy payments that didn't match any known projects."

Katherine tapped her foot. "You had him under surveillance."

"For six months." Chen's voice was still tight. "But three weeks before his death, Vanderlin made contact. He wanted to cooperate."

The pieces clicked into place. "He discovered the theft and came to you."

"More than that." Irvine leaned forward. "He provided evidence that someone at Meridian was systematically selling encrypted defense protocols to foreign nationals."

Katherine tilted her head. "Which gives us a completely different set of motives for his murder."

Chen nodded grimly. "Someone discovered he was cooperating. We believe his death was meant to silence him before he could testify."

"Professional hit?" Katherine asked.

"No." Chen's response was immediate. "The execution was too personal. A professional would never have used the victim's wife's gun or staged it in such an obvious way."

The implication hit Katherine like cold water. "Anna Bovill."

Chen's expression confirmed her suspicion. "Executive assistants to CFOs have access to sensitive financial information. She's been with Meridian for ten years, staying in that role because James trusted her completely. Too completely."

"And she has clearance for classified materials," Katherine added, seeing the pattern.

"Plus, access to James's calendar, his travel schedules, his meetings with us." Chen opened another folder. "We believe she's been selling information for years, using her position of trust to access trade secrets. But nothing flagged until the CFIUS review alerted us to suspicious activity."

Katherine studied the timeline forming in her mind. "Could she have hired someone? Made it look amateur to throw you off?"

Irvine shook his head. "We've had her accounts under surveillance since the investigation began. No unusual transfers, no payments to unknown parties. If she did this, she acted alone."

"And used Misty's gun to frame her," Katherine concluded.

"The perfect patsy," Chen agreed. "A jealous wife with means, motive, and opportunity."

Katherine crossed her arms. "Anna would have known about James's affair with Beth. Could have manipulated the situation to ensure Misty was at the museum at the right time."

"We think so." Irvine's tone carried a warning. "But proving it is another matter entirely. Anna Bovill has been operating under our noses for years, using James's complete trust in her to access and sell classified information. She's been careful, methodical. But murder? That's desperation."

Katherine paused before responding. "There's something else you need to know. My team examined the museum's new security system, the one James donated."

Chen looked up sharply. "What did you find?"

"Someone deliberately modified the camera angles during installation to create a perfect blind path from the service entrance to the Baroque gallery. We're talking professional operational security."

Irvine leaned forward. "Who installed the system?"

"A technician named Gavin Tucker, working off designs by Kyle Bovill. But we also discovered that Beth Taylor, James's pregnant lover, was taking shooting lessons with him. She's proficient with a Glock 19, same model as Misty's gun."

Chen narrowed his eyes. "You think she's involved?"

"I thought so. I spoke to her yesterday. She insisted on meeting this morning. Said she had information to share about Misty." Katherine's voice grew quiet. "When I arrived at her house at 9 AM, I found her body."

The men were speechless for a moment.

"Beth Taylor is dead?" Irvine couldn't mask his look of surprise.

Chen was already reaching for his phone. "We need a crime scene team to—"

"Already processed," Katherine interrupted. "I called it in immediately. Single gunshot. Just like James Vanderlin. And gentlemen, there's more. Baltimore PD found James Vanderlin's gun next to her body, the one that matches his wife's. Wiped clean. It looks like whoever's behind this is cleaning house. First James when he started cooperating with you, now Beth before she could talk to me."

Irvine stood, pacing to the window. "Anna Bovill?"

"That would be my guess. She had access to James's gun, knew about the affair, and would have realized Beth was becoming a liability." Katherine shifted in her seat. "The question is, who's next on her list?"

Chen stood as well. "Ms. Carson, if Anna is eliminating witnesses, you and your team could be targets. This isn't a game anymore."

"It never was," Katherine replied, standing to her feet. "But now we know we're dealing with someone willing to commit multiple murders to protect her operation. That changes everything."

"Be careful, Kat," Irvine said from the window. "Whatever she's done, she's covered her tracks."

"Except for one thing," Katherine said, moving toward the door. "She didn't count on us looking beyond the obvious suspect."

Chen stood as well. "Ms. Carson, if you're planning to confront her—"

"I'm planning to build a case that will free my client." Katherine paused at the threshold. "Thanks for the briefing, gentlemen. This has been ... illuminating."

As she walked back through the government corridors, Katherine's mind catalogued the new information. Anna Bovill—trusted assistant, long-term spy, possible killer. Someone with the access to betray defense secrets and the desperation to kill when threatened with exposure.

The elevator carried her down to street level where the Washington afternoon felt suddenly sharper, more dangerous. Katherine pulled out her phone to call Jake. A new suspect had risen to the top of the list.

But first, they had to prove that Anna Bovill was capable of murder.

26

The January cold bit through Jake's jacket as he stepped out of his Jeep onto 14th Street. Washington buzzed with an electric energy he hadn't felt in years. Crowds flowed toward the Capital. Vendors hawked Obama memorabilia. The air was thick with anticipation and exhaust fumes.

Jake pulled up the photo on his phone—stocky kid with glasses and nervous eyes. Twenty-three years old, according to SecureTech's employee records. Maryland University graduate, IT help desk since high school. The type who'd camp out for hours to catch a glimpse of history.

Jake started with the address SecureTech had on file, a group house near George Washington University. The guy who answered the door looked like he'd been awake for three straight days.

"Gavin? Yeah, he crashed here Sunday night. Or was it Monday?" The kid scratched his stubble, eyes bloodshot. "Dude, I honestly can't remember. We've been celebrating since like ... when did Obama get elected?"

"That was in November. It's January now."

"Right. Time flies when you're making history, man."

Jake showed him the photo. "When did you last see him?"

"Tuesday? Wednesday?"

"Today is Wednesday," Jake said with a sigh.

"Sorry, dude, my brain's fried. He said something about meeting up with his Maryland crew somewhere downtown."

Jake's next stop was a coffee shop where the barista thought she'd seen Gavin but couldn't be sure. Then a bar where the bartender insisted Gavin had been there but described someone who looked nothing like him.

Jake tried three more addresses from Gavin's social media check-ins. Each stop brought the same story. Yes, Gavin had been there. No, nobody could pin down exactly when, and everyone was too wasted to remember details.

At a basement apartment near Dupont Circle, a girl with Obama campaign buttons covering her jacket squinted at the photo.

"Oh yeah, Gavin! Super sweet guy. He was explaining how the surveillance cameras work for crowd control yesterday during the inauguration. Really fascinating stuff." She swayed gently, pupils dilated. "We're still celebrating, you know? Historic day and all. Wait, are you his dad?"

"When did you see him?"

"Last night? This morning? Honestly, it's all blending together. He mentioned going to meet some computer friends. Said something about Murphy's Pub having good Wi-Fi."

Jake pocketed his phone and surveyed the street. Four hours of chasing ghosts through a city still buzzing from yesterday's celebrations. His military training had taught him patience, but today it was wearing it thin.

Murphy's Pub was his eighth stop. The bouncer looked at the photo and nodded slowly.

"Chubby white kid? Yeah, he was here yesterday with some Maryland University crowd. Real chatty about computer stuff." The bouncer gestured toward the back. "But that crew moved on hours ago. Try O'Malley's down the block. That's where the college kids end up when they want to get seriously messed up."

O'Malley's reeked of stale beer and bad decisions. The front room pulsed with music and bodies pressed against each other. Jake pushed through, scanning faces, showing the photo to anyone who'd look.

"Back room," a bartender finally said, pointing toward a dimly lit corridor. "But I'd be careful back there if I were you."

Jake followed the narrow hallway past restrooms that smelled like vomit. The back room opened into a smaller space where smoke hung thick despite the no-smoking laws. Couches arranged in clusters; groups of kids who'd clearly started celebrating early and hadn't stopped.

He found Gavin slumped in the corner booth, head tilted back against cracked vinyl. His glasses hung crooked off one ear, and his Maryland University sweatshirt was covered in stains Jake didn't want to identify. The kid's mouth hung open, a line of drool trailing down his chin.

On Gavin's left, a girl with purple streaks in her hair had passed out against his shoulder. On his right, a guy in a Nationals cap stared at the ceiling, pupils dilated to black pools.

Jake approached slowly, hands visible. In his experience, stoned kids could be unpredictable.

"Gavin Tucker?"

The kid's eyes rolled toward him, unfocused and glassy. His head lolled forward like he was trying to nod, but no words came out.

"I'm Jake Mercer, private detective." Jake kept his voice calm and steady. "I need to talk to you about the Walters Museum."

Gavin blinked slowly, his mouth moving soundlessly. Whatever he'd taken had him floating somewhere beyond reach.

"Dude," the guy in the Nationals cap slurred, "he's been like that for hours. Can't even remember his own name."

Jake leaned closer. "Gavin, do you remember installing cameras? Security work?"

The kid's eyes tried to focus, but it was like watching someone look through fog. His lips moved, forming shapes that might have been words, but nothing coherent emerged.

"What about Anna Bovill? Do you know that name?"

A flicker crossed Gavin's face. His head bobbed slightly, and he managed to mumble, "Pretty... really pretty..."

But when Jake pressed for more about blueprints, camera angles, or anything useful, Gavin just stared at him with that same vacant expression.

The girl with purple hair stirred, blinking at Jake. "Who are you?"

"Someone who needs to take your friend home." Jake stood, assessing the situation. The kid was in no condition to walk, much less provide testimony.

"You can't just take him," she protested weakly.

Jake pulled out his identification. "He's needed for a murder inquiry in Baltimore. Official business."

The word 'murder' had the desired effect. The girl's eyes widened, and she shrank back into the booth. The guy in the Nationals cap suddenly found the ceiling even more interesting.

Jake slipped his arms under Gavin's shoulders and hoisted him up. The kid was dead weight, his head rolling against Jake's chest. A few other patrons glanced over, but when Jake met their eyes with the steady stare of someone accustomed to being obeyed, they looked away.

"If anyone asks," Jake announced to the room, "Gavin Tucker is needed for questioning in a homicide investigation. Any problems with that?"

Silence.

Jake half-carried, half-dragged Gavin through the narrow hallway, past the bartender who took one look at Jake's expression and decided not to ask questions. The cold D.C. air hit them like a slap as Jake maneuvered his limp burden toward his Jeep.

Gavin's head lolled back, and he mumbled something that might have been "inauguration" or might have been nonsense. His eyes rolled back, showing mostly whites.

Jake opened the back door and carefully deposited Gavin inside, buckling the seatbelt around him like he was securing cargo. The kid immediately slumped against the window.

As Jake climbed into the driver's seat, he glanced at his watch. Katherine's meeting with the FBI would be wrapping up soon, and they were no closer to getting the testimony they needed.

27

At the Carson Investigations office, Sammi and Lee sat surrounded by printouts, public records, and laptop screens displaying employment databases and social media profiles. The January wind rattled the windows, making Lee pull his sweater tighter around his shoulders.

"Gavin Tucker is totally broke," Sammi announced, dropping another stack of public employment records onto the table. "Seriously, Lee, this guy's financial situation is just depressing."

Lee glanced up from his laptop screen, where he'd been cross-referencing credit reporting agencies and public debt records. "Sometimes boring is exactly what we're looking for. The cleanest records often hide the dirtiest secrets."

"Yeah, but this isn't suspicious. It's just sad." Sammi waved her hands over the papers spread before them. "Salary at SecureTech that's barely above minimum wage, public records showing student loan debt in collections, credit reports showing maxed-out cards. The guy's LinkedIn shows he's been applying for other work for months with no luck."

"Poor kid's drowning in debt." Lee leaned back in his chair, studying the younger detective's frustrated expression. "Thirty-seven thousand in student loans according to the federal database. His credit score is in the tank. This doesn't look like someone with extra income to hide."

Sammi pulled up another social media profile on her laptop. "Look at this Instagram post from last week. He's literally eating ramen again and joking about being too broke for anything else. This guy couldn't afford to be part of some conspiracy even if he wanted to be."

"Sometimes ruling people out is just as valuable as ruling them in." Lee's voice carried gentle understanding.

"But that doesn't feel helpful." Sammi stared at her screen. "Everyone else is chasing actual leads."

Lee closed his laptop to give Sammi his full attention. She'd been pushing herself hard since joining the team last year, always trying to prove she belonged. Always trying to make the breakthrough that would cement her value.

"You know, eliminating false leads is real detective work." He stretched, his back protesting the hours of huddling over public records databases. "You're doing good work here, Sammi. Real good."

"I haven't found anything useful." Her voice carried the sharp edge of self-criticism. "Katherine's out there meeting with the FBI, Jake's tracking down actual leads in D.C., and I'm here staring at employment records and social media posts."

Lee recognized the expression on her face and the desperate need to prove worth through achievement. He'd worn it himself once, a long time ago.

The difference was, her mistakes were still theoretical. His were written in blood, locked away in classified NSA vaults where they'd stay forever. Every call he'd made that cost lives—those weren't hypotheticals. Those ghosts followed him to this very office every morning.

"Can I tell you something?" he asked quietly. "Something I wish someone had told me when I was your age?"

Sammi looked up from her screen. "Sure."

"You're valuable to this team because of who you are, not what you accomplish." Lee spoke with the authority of his hard-earned wisdom. "Katherine didn't hire you because she needed someone to crack cases. She hired you because she saw something in you. Your integrity, your perspective, your instincts."

"But if I can't contribute—"

"You are contributing," Lee interrupted gently. "Every question you ask, every fresh angle you bring, every time you challenge our assumptions, that's contribution. You don't have to solve every case to matter."

Sammi was quiet for a moment, her fingers absently tracing the edge of an employment verification form. "It's just ... everyone else has this history, you know? Military, espionage, national security. I'm just some kid from Puerto Rico with a criminal justice degree."

"Just some kid?" Lee's eyebrows raised. "Garcia, you spotted the connection between the motive and the security installation when the rest of us missed it. You identified Beth Taylor at the gun club when everyone else was chasing the wrong lead. You figured out the phone records angle that's about to crack this case wide open."

"Those were lucky breaks."

"Those were good detective work. Pattern recognition. Fresh eyes seeing what experienced ones missed."

Sammi finally met his gaze. "How do you stay confident when everything feels uncertain?"

Lee rubbed his chin, resting his elbow on the desk. "Truth is, I don't always. I spent a lot of years defining myself by my mistakes." He paused, looking out the window at the gray Baltimore afternoon. "I let my past write my story for too long."

A familiar weight settled in his chest—faces he couldn't forget, decisions he'd replay forever. That operation in Prague where his miscalculation cost lives. The asset he'd failed to extract from Moscow because he'd trusted the wrong intel. Every wrong call, every moment of hesitation that led to consequences he'd carry until his dying day. Even now, Katherine and Jake trusted him with their lives, and some mornings he woke up wondering if he deserved that faith.

"What changed?"

"Katherine, actually." Lee smiled at the memory. "When we first started this agency seven years ago, I was just caught up in proving I wasn't the screwup my NSA record suggested. So caught up, I nearly missed a crucial piece of evidence on our first case. Kat pulled me aside afterward and said something that stuck: 'I didn't choose you as a partner because of your past. I chose you because of your future '."

Sammi smiled. "She said that?"

"She did. And she was right." Lee leaned forward, his expression earnest. "I can't change my past, kid, but you can damn well change your future. Don't let the pressure to prove yourself make you miss what's right in front of you."

If only it were that simple for him. Maybe helping Sammi avoid his mistakes was worth something. Maybe preventing her from carrying the weight he carried was a kind of redemption.

Sammi looked down at the employment records and public information scattered across the table, seeing them with new eyes. "You're saying confirming Gavin's financial situation is actually valuable information?"

"I'm saying you've been looking at this exactly right." Lee nodded encouragingly. "A broke college kid drowning in student debt doesn't have the resources or motivation to be part of an elaborate murder conspiracy."

"So we can rule him out completely."

"Now you're thinking like a detective." Lee reopened his laptop. "Which means we need to focus our attention on the people who do have means and motive."

Sammi's energy returned. "You're right. If someone used Gavin's access, they manipulated him without his knowledge. He's a victim, not a suspect."

"There's that fresh perspective Katherine hired you for."

"You think we should report back that Gavin's clean?"

"I think you just eliminated a major distraction from our investigation." His phone buzzed with an incoming text. He glanced at the screen, then looked up at Sammi with a grin. "Well, speak of the devil."

"What is it?"

"Katherine. Says they found Gavin and they're driving back from D.C." His eyebrows raised as he continued reading. "Apparently, he's not in a condition to be interviewed just yet."

Sammi leaned forward. "What do you mean?"

"Let's just say our broke college student found a way to spend his limited funds on recreational activities." Lee set his phone down. "Katherine says they'll be back in two hours, and we should probably have coffee ready. Strong coffee."

"So we still need to talk to him."

"Absolutely. Just because he's not guilty doesn't mean he doesn't have answers." Lee's voice grew more serious. "Someone used his access to sabotage that security system. We need to know how, and more importantly, who convinced him to give them that access."

28

Lee adjusted his collar against the Baltimore wind. Detective Eden was already waiting for him outside the precinct, steam rising from her coffee cup in the frigid afternoon air.

"What've you got for me, Stewart?"

Lee handed the police detective a thick file folder. "Anna Bovill. Twelve years as James Vanderlin's executive assistant. Access to everything from his calendar to his office safe." He paused, meeting her eyes. "And according to Owen Lacroix, she's one of only two people who knew the combination to James's gun safe."

"The other being James himself."

"Right. But here's where it gets interesting. FBI's Economic Espionage Unit has been building a case on Meridian Tech for months. Someone's been selling classified defense algorithms, but they can't prove it yet."

Rhonda studied the financial records. "And you think it's Anna?"

"We reckon it fits. She's had access to sensitive information for over a decade. Knows the company inside and out, understands what's valuable." Lee stuffed his gloved hands into his coat pockets. "Plus, she's got a solid motive now. James was cooperating with the feds. If he figured out what she was doing..."

"She'd lose her golden goose." Rhonda straightened up. "What about the wife? Misty's still our primary suspect."

"Security footage doesn't lie, but it can be manipulated. The camera upgrades were installed by Gavin Tucker, a young man who worked for Anna's husband. With Gavin's help, she could've orchestrated the whole thing. And having access to James Vanderlin's gun means she should be your prime suspect for the Beth Taylor murder. Misty couldn't have pulled that trigger," Lee shot her his best lopsided grin, "she was in your detention center at the time."

Rhonda drained her coffee and tossed the cup in a nearby trash bin. "Alright, hon. Let's go have a conversation with Ms. Bovill."

The arrest happened at the Bovills' well-appointed rowhouse in Federal Hill. Anna Bovill answered the door in a cream cashmere sweater and pressed slacks, looking like she was dressed for a business meeting rather than a Wednesday evening at home. She peered out at Rhonda and the two uniformed officers on her front steps.

"Ms. Bovill? I'm Detective Eden, Baltimore PD. I need you to come with us for questioning regarding the murders of James Vanderlin and Beth Taylor."

Anna's posture stiffened immediately. "I've already spoken with investigators about James's death."

"New information has come to light." Rhonda gestured toward the patrol car parked at the curb. "You have the right to remain silent..."

Lee watched from the sidewalk as Anna's expression went from surprise to resignation. She didn't protest or ask questions. Just stepped back into the foyer to gather her purse and coat with the same methodical efficiency she probably brought to everything else.

❧

Lee was reviewing his notes when Agent Chen appeared beside him, looking about as happy as a cat in a thunderstorm.

"Stewart." Chen's voice was clipped, professional anger barely contained. "What the hell do you think you're doing?"

"Well, hey there to you too," Lee drawled, not looking up from his notes. "I reckon we're investigating a murder. Last I checked, that was still legal in Baltimore."

"You just arrested our primary suspect in a federal investigation."

Lee finally looked up, meeting Chen's glare with practiced calm. "Y'all been investigating her for months and haven't made a move. We've got two bodies and a woman in lockup for crimes she didn't commit."

"We're building an airtight case—"

"While people die." Lee's voice hardened. "Look, I get it. Federal cases take time. But we've got evidence linking Anna to the murder weapon, and that's leverage you don't have on the espionage front."

Chen's jaw tightened. "What evidence?"

"Access to James's gun safe. Opportunity during the security system upgrade. Motive if James was getting too close to her operation." Lee shrugged. "Maybe she doesn't confess to treason, but if she's looking at life for murder..."

"She might trade information for a plea deal." Chen's expression shifted, calculation replacing anger. "The murder charge could give us the pressure we need."

"Exactly. Y'all suspect she's your spy, but you can't prove it. We suspect she's our killer, and we've got more to work with." Lee gestured toward the interrogation room. "Work together instead of against each other."

Chen was quiet for a long moment, then nodded curtly. "I want to observe the questioning."

"You'll have to take that up with Rhonda. This is still her case."

Lee and Agent Chen watched through the one-way glass as Rhonda sat across from Anna in the interrogation room. Anna's hands were folded precisely in her lap, her back straight, every inch the composed executive assistant.

"Ms. Bovill," Rhonda began, sliding a folder across the metal table. "We have questions about James Vanderlin's murder. But I think we both know this goes deeper than that."

Anna's eyes flicked to the folder, but she didn't open it. "I'd like to speak with an attorney."

"That's your right. But I'm curious. Why kill James if he was your source of information? Seems counterproductive."

"I didn't kill James." The words came out measured, precise. "That would be foolish. Why would I eliminate my access?"

Behind the glass, Chen leaned forward. "She's right. It doesn't make sense from an espionage perspective."

Rhonda continued. "Maybe because your access was about to be eliminated anyway. James was cooperating with federal investigators. How long before he figured out you were the leak?"

A muscle in Anna's jaw twitched. "James didn't know anything about the business side. He was brilliant with technology, but operations? Strategy? That was all me."

"So there was information being sold."

A long pause. Anna stared at the wall behind Rhonda's head, choosing her words carefully. "I wouldn't know anything about that."

Lee shook his head. "She's not going to admit to federal crimes."

Chen's phone buzzed. He checked it and frowned. "My supervisor wants Anna transferred to federal custody for questioning about the espionage case."

"Not happening," Lee said flatly. "Not until we clear the murders."

"This isn't a negotiation—"

"Actually, it is." Rhonda's voice came through the intercom. She was looking directly at the mirror. "Ms. Bovill, we have evidence placing you with access to the murder weapon. We know you had the opportunity to manipulate the security system. And we know James's cooperation with federal authorities gave you motive."

Anna's composure finally slipped. "You think I stayed there for him? That's what everyone thinks. They think I was so in love with James that I was his executive assistant for all these years, for the same lousy pay, the same lousy, under-appreciated job."

She laughed sharply, the sound cutting through the room's tension. "He didn't know anything about business. I was running that office, and while I was doing it..." She stopped abruptly, as if realizing she'd said too much.

"While you were doing what, Anna?"

Anna straightened up, walls slamming back into place. "I want that attorney now."

29

Katherine stared out at the passing landscape as Jake's Jeep cut through the evening traffic. Behind them, Gavin Tucker was sprawled across the back seat, unconscious after Jake had forced two bottles of water and a sleeve of crackers into him.

"How long until he's coherent enough to talk to us?" Katherine asked.

"Few more hours. I've seen worse." Jake glanced in the rearview mirror. "Kid's going to have a nasty hangover, but he'll be functional by morning."

The rhythmic hum of tires on asphalt filled the silence. Katherine pulled out her phone to check messages, then put it away without reading them. Too much information to process all at once. She was still thinking about her meeting with the FBI.

A groan from the back seat made her turn around. Gavin's eyes fluttered open, unfocused and confused.

"Where..." His voice was hoarse, barely audible. "Where are we going?"

"Baltimore," Katherine said in her best motherly tone. "You're going to help us with a case at the Walters Art Museum."

Gavin blinked slowly, trying to focus on the passing highway signs. "Oh, never been there 'fore." The words slurred together. "Always meant to ... Heard they ... nice paintings."

His eyes closed again, and his breathing returned to the deep rhythm of sleep.

Katherine and Jake exchanged glances.

"Curious," she murmured. "Several witnesses place him at the museum."

"He's wasted. May not know what he's saying." Jake rolled his eyes dramatically. "Tell me how your meeting went."

Katherine was quiet for a moment, organizing her thoughts. "Greg was good. Glad to see me. He ordered Chen to give me a full briefing."

Jake chuckled. "I bet Chen was thrilled about that!"

Katherine smiled. "Yeah, I let him have it a little myself. Name dropped a few of my credentials."

"Okay! Look at you playing the expert card! I can imagine the look on Chen's face."

Katherine let herself giggle. "It actually felt pretty good to flex a little."

Jake nodded. "That's great. Did you get what you came for?"

"Yeah, I did. Confirmed our guess that Anna Bovill is their prime suspect at Meridian Tech. James was working with them."

Jake whistled. "That gives her an even stronger motive for murder."

"They are starting to believe Misty's story that she didn't know anything about James's business dealings, but they are interested in Sammi's idea that he could have let something slip to Beth."

"How'd they take the news about Beth's murder?"

"They were pretty taken aback. I don't think they saw that coming, even after James's murder."

"You think the espionage is connected to the deaths?"

Katherine glanced at Gavin sleeping in the back seat.

"Somehow I don't think so. There are some details that look professional, like the camera setup. But all in all, the whole thing seems badly planned. Like someone was too emotional to follow through with the cover up."

"Doesn't sound like a pro."

"Now, Greg did have some good info for me about our other case. They've been tracking Quinn Pham for months as part of a larger art theft investigation. Rumors suggest he's been fencing stolen pieces from galleries and museums on the East Coast, but they don't have solid connections."

"Nothing they can prove in court."

"Not yet." Katherine looked back at the darkened road. "Greg was very interested in Harold Cartwright's money laundering operation, and his successor, Christopher Euler. More interested than I thought he'd be."

"How interested?"

"Enough to ask me to stay undercover as Samantha Casey while they ferret out Euler's other contacts."

The sound of the highway took over for a few minutes. Jake's expression was unreadable in the dim light from the dashboard.

"And?" he finally asked.

"And what?"

"Are you considering it?"

Katherine turned to study his profile. "You sound surprised."

"I am. But also pleased." Jake's voice carried an undertone she couldn't quite identify. "It's good work, Katie. Important work."

She was about to respond when her phone rang. Lee's name appeared on the display. "Hey, Lee, you're on speaker."

"Anna Bovill's been arrested. Police picked her up about two hours ago on suspicion of murdering Beth Taylor."

"That's good news for Misty."

"Well, yes and no." Lee's voice carried a note of caution. "Anna almost confessed to the espionage charges, but she caught herself and called a lawyer. Now she's completely shut down."

Katherine closed her eyes. "Of course she is."

"Gets worse. Agent Chen made it to Baltimore, and he's furious about us getting involved with his suspect. Anna's flatly denying having anything to do with either murder. Claims she was at a fundraising event on Friday night when James was killed, and out for dinner with friends when Beth was murdered."

Jake's hands tightened on the steering wheel. "Convenient alibis."

"The police are verifying her story, but early indications suggest she is actually be telling the truth about where she was," Lee said. "Problem is, if she's got solid alibis for both nights, we're back to square one on the murders."

Katherine leaned her head back against the headrest. "And square one puts our client back in the frame."

30

Lee found Detective Eden at her desk, pecking away at a computer keyboard.

"Paperwork?" he asked, settling into the chair in front of her desk.

"Reports on the Bovill arrest. FBI's breathing down our necks, wanting everything documented before they try to snatch her away." Rhonda looked up from the screen. "What's on your mind, hon?"

"Paul Zabala. The shipping manager at the museum." Lee pulled out his notepad. "Remember he was in the loading area when those crates nearly turned Katherine and me into pancakes?"

"Hard to forget. You think he was involved?"

"I reckon he's worth a look. Man's awfully protective of Misty, and he sure didn't seem to care much for Beth Taylor." Lee flipped through his notes. "Plus, he had access to the loading area, knows the museum's layout better than most."

Rhonda minimized her report and pulled up the department's database. "Let's see what we can find. Paul Anthony Zabala..." She typed rapidly. "Clean record. Couple of parking tickets, nothing serious."

"What about employment history?"

"Been at the Walters for... eighteen years. Started as a general maintenance worker, worked his way up to shipping manager." Rhonda frowned at the screen. "That's interesting."

"What?"

"His salary records. Base pay of forty-eight thousand, but look at these quarterly payments." She pointed to the monitor. "Additional payments of twenty-five hundred every three months, labeled as 'performance bonuses'."

Lee leaned closer. "That seem normal to you?"

"Hell no. My sister Denise works at the American Visionary Art Museum downtown. Museums don't give bonuses, especially not quarterly ones. They're nonprofits—every penny goes back into operations or acquisitions." Rhonda scrolled through more records. "These payments go back at least three years."

"Sounds like Paul's been getting paid for more than shipping coordination."

Rhonda nodded, closing the window. "Question is, paid by who and for what?"

"We need to talk to Paul again," Lee told Rhonda. "But this time, we ask harder questions."

"Agreed. Soon as we finish with Anna Bovill." Rhonda glanced toward the interrogation rooms. "Speaking of which, her lawyer just arrived. This should be interesting."

"Federal agents here yet?"

"Agent Chen's been lurking in the hallway. I think he's waiting to see if we can break her on the murder charges before he makes his move."

Lee grinned. "Well then, let's go see if we can give him what he's waiting for."

Lee needed air. The interrogation room felt like a pressure cooker, and Agent Chen's federal jurisdiction posturing wasn't helping his mood any. He wandered down to the precinct's main lobby, rolling his shoulders to work out the tension.

Kyle Bovill sat in one of the hard plastic chairs near the front desk, hands in his pockets, whistling "Don't Rain on My Parade." He wore a heavy wool coat and designer jeans, looking completely out of place among the usual collection of bail bondsmen and worried relatives.

"Mr. Bovill?" Lee approached cautiously. "What brings you down here?"

Kyle jumped up immediately, his hands starting to move in animated gestures. "Oh! Mr. Stewart, correct? I was hoping— well, you see, I heard about Anna being brought in and I thought, rhetorical question, really, shouldn't a husband be here for his wife?"

"That's ... thoughtful of you." Lee studied Kyle's face. The man's eyes darted around the lobby like he was cataloging every security camera and exit. "You wanting to post bail or just visit?"

"I—well—you see—the thing is ..." Kyle started over, speaking faster. "I don't really know what she's been charged with. The officer at the desk was very unclear. Could you maybe explain what exactly Anna is supposed to have done?"

"She's being questioned in connection with James Vanderlin's murder."

"Murder?" Kyle's voice pitched higher with what seemed like genuine surprise. "That's ridiculous! Anna would never—she couldn't hurt anyone! She's been devastated by James's death. Absolutely devastated!"

His hands gestured wildly as he spoke, almost knocking over a promotional display for Crime Stoppers. "I mean, they worked together for twelve years! Friends since high school. She knew him better than anyone, except maybe Misty, and we all know Misty's the one who—"

"Actually," Lee interrupted, "we're also looking into some federal charges. Corporate espionage."

Kyle stopped mid-gesture. His face went completely pale. "Corporate ... what?"

"Espionage. Selling classified information." Lee watched Kyle's reaction carefully. "Someone's been leaking trade secrets from Meridian Tech for years."

"I—" Kyle's mouth opened and closed soundlessly. His hands dropped to his sides. "Anna? You think Anna is ... but that's impossible. She's just an executive assistant. She doesn't have access to—I mean, she wouldn't know how to—" He stopped abruptly.

"Wouldn't know how to what, Mr. Bovill?"

"Nothing. I just—this is all very confusing." Kyle backed toward the door. "Maybe I should speak with a lawyer first. Before I talk to Anna. Yes, that's what I should do."

"You don't need a lawyer to visit your wife."

"No, no, I think," Kyle was already pulling out his car keys, hands shaking slightly, "I should go. This is all very ... I need to think about this." He paused at the door, turning back with a strained smile. "She didn't kill James, Detective. I know Anna, and she's not capable of murder. But the other thing ..." He shook his head. "I just don't understand how that's possible."

Before Lee could respond, Kyle was gone, practically running across the parking lot to his Audi.

31

Katherine pushed through the office door, Jake right behind her with Gavin Tucker's unconscious form slung over his shoulder. Whatever cocktail of substances he'd consumed in D.C. had left him limp as a rag doll.

Lee looked up from his computer. "What did he take?"

"Half the pharmacy, from the smell of it." Jake deposited Gavin on the couch, checking his pulse. "He'll live, but he won't be answering questions for a while."

Sammi bounced up from her chair. "How was the FBI meeting?"

Katherine hung her coat on a hook by the door. "Anna Bovill has been selling trade secrets for years. James was cooperating with the feds, so she must have killed him to protect her operation."

"That's the working theory." Lee leaned back in his chair. "But police confirmed Anna's alibi for the night James Vanderlin was killed."

"She was at a charity fundraising event," Sammi spread her hands wide, "with a room full of witnesses."

"What about Beth Taylor's death?" Jake asked.

"They are still tracking down the friends she had dinner with," Sammi replied. "But it doesn't look promising for us."

"Kyle Bovill showed up at the station, supposedly to support his wife, but ..." Lee paused, scratching his head. "Something felt off. When I mentioned the murder charges, he seemed surprised, not worried. But the espionage thing? He went white as a sheet."

Katherine leaned forward. "You'd think a husband would be worried about a murder charge."

"Unless he knows she isn't guilty," Jake commented.

"More than that." Sammi pulled her chair closer to the group. "We've been thinking about Kyle's alibi for the night James was murdered. It's almost too perfect."

"Walk me through it." Katherine settled back.

Lee consulted his notes. "Kyle claims he was home alone, working on renovations until late. Says he lost track of time and kept running a table saw after 8:00 PM. Neighbor filed a noise complaint. Police called his house at 8:28 PM and spoke to Kyle directly. He apologized, said he'd stop immediately."

"Thirty-minute drive to the museum," Jake observed. "No way he makes it there by 8:40 PM."

"Unless he wasn't actually home when he answered that call." Sammi's eyes lit up with the thrill of discovery. "We know Kyle designed the security system at the museum, right?"

Katherine nodded. "He'd know exactly how to manipulate those cameras. What are you thinking?"

Lee stood up, energized. "Call forwarding. Kyle could have set his home line to forward to his cell. When the police called the house, it rang his cell phone instead."

"But what about the neighbor hearing the saw?" Jake's skepticism was practical.

"Timer switch." Sammi was on her feet now, pacing with excitement. "Or even a simple outlet timer. Set the saw to turn on at intervals, maybe with a piece of wood positioned to make it sound like active work."

Katherine closed her eyes, visualizing the timeline. "He sets up the noise machine, forwards his phone, drives to the museum. When the police call at 8:28 PM, he's already there. Answers casually, apologizes for the 'noise,' hangs up, and has twelve minutes to execute the murder and frame Misty."

"It's brilliant," Lee admitted grudgingly. "Low-tech solution to create a high-tech alibi."

Jake was shaking his head. "It's theoretically possible, but can we prove it works?"

"We test it." Katherine opened her eyes. "Right here."

Lee frowned. "We don't exactly have a table saw lying around."

"Hardware store's still open." Jake checked his watch. "I can grab a circular saw and some lumber. What else do we need?"

"Timer switch, extension cord, and a landline phone." Katherine stood up. "Sammi, can you set up call forwarding on our office line?"

"Easy. Route it to one of our cells."

An hour later, their office looked like a construction site. Jake had returned with a basic circular saw, several pieces of two-by-four, and an assortment of electrical equipment. The saw sat on Katherine's desk, extension cord snaking to a timer switch plugged into the wall.

"This is the problem." Jake examined the saw's safety features. "Most modern tools have deadman switches. You have to hold the trigger down for them to run."

Lee was studying the manual. "Says here it has a safety lock to prevent accidental startup."

"Kyle would know about this," Sammi observed. "He works with power tools all the time."

Katherine picked up the saw, testing the trigger mechanism. "There has to be a way to bypass it."

Jake found a roll of duct tape in their supply closet. "This stuff fixes everything." He wrapped tape around the trigger, holding it in the depressed position.

"That's not going to work with the safety lock," Lee pointed out.

Sammi was examining the side of the saw. "Look! There's a lock button here. If you press it while holding the trigger, it stays engaged until you release the trigger."

"So tape the trigger down, engage the lock, then the timer just controls the power." Katherine watched as Jake worked. "When the timer switches on, the saw runs automatically."

It took them twenty minutes of fiddling to get it right. The first attempt failed when the tape slipped. The second time, Jake hadn't engaged the safety lock properly. Finally, on the third try, they had success.

"Timer's set for thirty-second intervals," Sammi announced. "Starting, now!"

The saw roared to life, blade spinning against a piece of lumber positioned to create maximum noise. After thirty seconds, it shut off automatically.

"That's loud enough to wake the dead," Lee commented, covering his ears.

"And definitely loud enough for a neighbor to complain." Katherine felt satisfaction at seeing the theory proven. Her BlackBerry rang.

"Carson," she answered.

"The forwarding works perfectly," Sammi reported over the phone. "Caller ID shows the office number, not my cell."

Katherine looked at her desk where Lee was sitting by the phone with a big smile on his face. Sammi hurried back in the room and showed her the caller ID.

"You'd never know the call was forwarded," Sammi said.

Jake and Katherine exchanged looks. This might actually work.

"Kyle sets up the saw, programs the timer, and forwards his phone." Katherine laid out the sequence. "Drives to the museum, kills James and frames Misty. When the police call about the noise complaint, he's standing over James's body, but he answers like he's in his basement workshop."

"The neighbor hears the saw because it's actually running," Lee added. "Just nobody's operating it."

Sammi was photographing their improvised setup. "After he hangs up with the police, he has time to finish framing Misty, drive home, and shut off the timer before anyone thinks to check on him."

Jake settled back into his chair. "This is a good theory, but still just a theory. Was Kyle doing Anna's bidding, or did he have his own motive? And we still have the timeline issue at the museum. Misty didn't hear the gunshot, but she found her husband dead. How do we explain that?"

Katherine smiled. "Actually, I might have the answer for that one."

32

Sammi clutched a steaming mug of coffee in her hands. The warmth grounded her against the nervous energy in her chest. Katherine asked her to talk to Gavin. He was about her age, and Katherine said maybe Sammi could get through to him when they couldn't.

She sat on the edge of one of the office couches and set the mug on the coffee table. Across the table, Gavin slouched on the other couch, staring at the floor. His eyes were still glassy, but at least they were open. She cleared her throat, cautiously sliding the mug toward him.

"Black coffee," she said, her voice softer than she intended. "Figured it might help clear your head."

Gavin's gaze shifted to the cup, then to her. He took it with a smirk. "Thanks," he muttered, lifting it to his lips.

Sammi looked over her shoulder, to the other end of the room where her teammates were huddled around a computer. She didn't have years of experience or a badge. But Katherine believed in her. That had to count for something.

"So ... D.C., huh?" she began, trying to sound casual. "Bet it was pretty wild with the inauguration and all."

Gavin snorted, setting the cup down. "You could say that. Packed everywhere. People crying, cheering, chaos."

She smiled. "I would've loved to see it. First Black president in the White House? That's history. Gives you hope, you know?"

"Yeah, guess so." Gavin shrugged. But a smile was tugging at the corner of his lips. "He's got his work cut out for him, though. People are talking like he's supposed to fix the world overnight."

Sammi chuckled, relaxing slightly. "Yeah, well, people always want a miracle. I'm just glad to see someone who looks like me up there."

Gavin's eyes flicked toward her, taking in her light brown complexion. "Yeah, I get that. It was ... something else, being there. Energy like I've never felt before."

Encouraged by his response, Sammi leaned closer. "So, what made you decide to go? Work doesn't seem like it'd let you take off during a big job like the museum."

Gavin hesitated, running a hand through his hair. "I had some time saved up. Swapped assignments with Kyle. He said he'd cover for me so I could, y'know, take a break."

Sammi tilted her head, feigning casual interest. "That was nice of him. Bet the company wasn't thrilled about losing both of you, though."

"Nah, no one noticed," Gavin said, a touch too quickly. He sipped his coffee, avoiding her gaze. "Kyle, he's good with that stuff. Made sure things looked normal. You know, punching me in and out, covering my tracks. Nobody even asked."

Sammi kept her voice light. "Really? That's a pretty big favor. Must've been tough for him to juggle everything."

Gavin laughed. "Kyle's a smooth talker. He likes to ... make arrangements."

A switch clicked in her mind, and she leaned back slightly, letting the silence hang for a beat. "He must've really wanted you to go. I mean, swapping shifts and all. What was the rush?"

Gavin shifted uncomfortably in his seat. "Kyle said he had stuff to do. Wanted to hang around his girlfriend, I think. Said it was no big deal, just a couple of days here and there."

Sammi caught the slip. "A couple of days? I thought you said he was covering your whole trip."

Gavin froze, realizing his mistake. His eyes darted toward the door, then back to Sammi. "Look, it's ... it's not a big deal, okay? He handled it. Made it look like I was there, even when I wasn't."

Her heart raced, but she kept her tone even. "Handled it how? Did he go to the museum?"

Gavin's mouth opened, then closed. Finally, he groaned, rubbing his face with both hands. "Yeah, okay? He went. Did the work. Whatever. Said it'd be easier if I just stayed out of the way."

"Stayed out of the way for what, Gavin?"

He looked at her, his frustration melting into fear. "I don't know, okay? Kyle said it was nothing, just covering for me. But he's smart, you know? Gets into things. Computers, systems. He knows how to make stuff happen."

Sammi took a careful breath. "Gavin, this is important. Did Kyle ever say why he wanted you to leave town? Did he give you any reason at all?" Sammi felt a pang of guilt. Here was this kid, barely older than her, strung out and confused, and she was basically interrogating him. But if Kyle had used him ...

Gavin hesitated, then shrugged. "Said I'd thank him for it later. Free trip, historic moment, no questions asked. I didn't want to look a gift horse in the mouth."

Sammi nodded slowly, her mind racing. Kyle had arranged the young tech's absence and his own presence at the museum.

"Gavin, did Kyle ever talk about James Vanderlin?"

Gavin's face paled. "I don't know anything about that. I swear."

Sammi leaned forward, her voice firm but kind. "I believe you. But Kyle knows more than he's letting on. And we need to know the truth before it's too late."

He swallowed hard, gripping the coffee mug. "I didn't do anything. I swear."

"I know," Sammi said, her tone softening. "But you might've seen something. Or heard something. Anything could help."

Gavin stared at her for a long moment, then nodded, his shoulders sagging in defeat. "Fine. I'll tell you what I know. But you have to promise I'm not gonna get dragged into this mess."

Sammi gave him a reassuring smile, though her stomach churned with unease. He was already in this mess over his head. "Just tell me everything, Gavin. We'll figure it out."

33

The interrogation room felt smaller than it was, the fluorescent lights buzzing overhead. Katherine sat across from Anna Bovill, Margaret beside her with a legal pad covered in notes. Anna sat perfectly straight in her chair, but Katherine could see the telltale signs of strain. A slight tremor in her clasped hands, the way she blinked too often when the questions got sharp.

"Let's talk about Kyle," Katherine said without preamble. "His relationship with James. With Misty."

Anna's professional mask stayed in place, but her eyebrows drew together slightly. "What do you mean?"

"Kyle went to Misty. Told her about James and Beth. Used your confidence to try to destroy James's marriage." Katherine kept her gaze leveled directly at Anna.

For the first time, real emotion flickered across Anna's face. Surprise, then fury. "He what?"

Margaret leaned forward, voice oozing with honey. "You told Kyle about the affair in confidence, dear. And he ran straight to Misty with it."

Anna's composure cracked. "That manipulative bastard." The words came out low, venomous. "I told him that in our bedroom. James was struggling, feeling guilty about Beth, and I ..." She stopped, catching herself.

Katherine pounced. "You what? Still cared about him?"

Anna's hands clenched on the metal table. "James and I have a history."

"High school history," Margaret said. "You two were together then, weren't you?"

"For three years before ..." She gestured vaguely. "Before life got complicated."

"And Kyle?"

Anna's mouth twisted. "Kyle followed us around like a lost puppy. Always wanting what James had. Always jealous." Her voice carried years of frustration. "Even after James and I broke up, even after Kyle finally convinced me to marry him, he never stopped comparing himself to James."

Katherine studied Anna's face, noting the anger burning there. "Kyle's been in love with you for thirty years."

"Kyle's been obsessed with beating James for thirty years. I just happened to be part of the prize." The bitterness in Anna's voice cut through the stale air.

Margaret made a note, then looked up. "So when you told Kyle about the affair ..."

"I thought I was talking to my husband in confidence." Anna's voice rose slightly. "James was torn up about it. Said he was going to end things with Beth, recommit to Misty. He felt like he'd betrayed everything he believed in."

"But you never shared business information with Kyle," Margaret said carefully.

Anna's head snapped up. "Of course not. Kyle couldn't understand James's work if I drew him diagrams."

Katherine leaned forward. "But you were sharing business information with someone."

Anna's professional mask slid back into place, but her breathing had changed. "I don't know what you're implying."

"We know about the corporate espionage, Anna. The FBI's been watching."

Anna's face went white, but her voice stayed level. "I had nothing to do with James's death."

"Maybe not directly," Katherine said. "But James figured out what you were doing, didn't he? That's why he moved his gun."

"James was becoming paranoid about office security, yes. But I never—" Anna stopped, calculating.

Margaret's pen had stopped moving. "You never what, dear?"

"I never told Kyle anything about the business. Only personal matters. James's guilt, his marriage problems."

"But Kyle took that personal information and weaponized it," Katherine said.

"Of course he did." Anna's voice carried bitter resignation. "I should have known. Kyle's never been able to compete with James honestly, so he sabotages instead. The museum security contract, the—" She stopped abruptly.

"The what?" Margaret pressed.

Anna shook her head, trying to regain control. "Nothing. Kyle's business practices aren't my concern."

"Tell us about Kyle's alibi," Katherine urged. "The night James died."

Anna frowned. "He was home. Working on a project in the garage. The police called about a noise complaint around eight-thirty, and Kyle answered from home."

Katherine and Margaret exchanged glances. "Anna," Katherine began carefully, "we think Kyle rigged that alibi. Timer switches, call forwarding. Created the illusion he was home while he was actually at the museum."

Anna stared at them for a long moment, then laughed—a sharp, disbelieving sound. "Kyle? You think Kyle set up some elaborate scheme?" She shook her head. "He's not smart enough for something like that."

"But he is jealous enough," Katherine pressed. "Jealous enough to frame Misty for murder."

Anna's laughter died. "Kyle isn't a killer. He's petty, manipulative, but he's not—"

"He killed Beth Taylor too," Margaret said quietly.

The color drained from Anna's face. "Beth is dead?"

"One shot, close range." Katherine slid a picture of the Vanderlins' guns across the table. "Misty's gun killed James. And James's gun killed Beth."

Anna's hands began to shake. "When?"

"Yesterday morning. Right after she offered to tell us everything she knew about the case."

Anna closed her eyes. "Oh God. Kyle knew I was worried about the FBI investigation."

"What did you tell him?"

"I said James had suspected me of leaking information. That he'd moved his gun because he was afraid." Anna's voice became smaller. "I thought Kyle would be sympathetic. I thought … "

"You thought your husband would comfort you," Katherine finished. "Instead, he saw an opportunity."

"Kyle's always resented that James trusted me with important things. That I knew details about his life, his business, his marriage." She looked up at Katherine with dawning horror. "You really think Kyle could have planned all this?"

Katherine met her eyes steadily. "I think Kyle's been planning to destroy James Vanderlin for years. He just finally found the perfect way to do it."

Anna buried her face in her hands.

34

Lee spread six photographs across the small table in the museum's volunteer office. Eleanor Abernathy adjusted her reading glasses, peering down at the images of similar-looking men under fifty.

"Mrs. Abernathy, I want you to take your time. Look at each face carefully. Do any of these men look like the technician who installed the security system with Misty?"

Eleanor studied each photo methodically. When she reached the fourth image, Kyle Bovill, she paused.

"This one." She tapped Kyle's photograph. "Yes, this is him. I'm certain."

"You're sure it's not this man?" Lee pointed to Gavin Tucker's photo in the lineup.

"Oh no, definitely not. This one." She indicated Kyle again. "He was very polite, very professional. Knew exactly what he was doing with those cameras." Eleanor looked up at Lee. "Why? Is he in some kind of trouble?"

The Precision Point Shooting Range sat in a strip mall forty miles outside Richmond. Jake pushed through the glass door, ID already open.

"I'm Jake Mercer, a private detective. Need to ask about a customer."

The heavyset man straightened. "What customer?" His name tag identified him as Rick, the owner.

Jake slid Kyle's photo across the counter. "This man. Probably paid cash for training sessions."

The owner studied the image. "Yeah, Kyle something. Came in six, seven times over eighteen months. Advanced marksmanship training."

"What days?"

"Tuesdays and Wednesdays, always weekday afternoons. Said he was corporate security, needed to stay sharp." He pulled out an appointment book. "Thing is, guy said he was rusty, but his fundamentals were solid from day one."

"What weapon?"

"Always rented Glock 19s. Wanted to get comfortable with that specific model."

"How comfortable did he get?" Jake raised his eyebrows.

"By his last visit—December fifteenth—he was putting tight groups at fifty yards. Takes serious skill."

Three weeks before the murder.

Jake showed Anna's photo. "Ever see this woman?"

"Never. Always came alone."

Jake made notes. Kyle's travel records had led him to Richmond. Regular Tuesday and Wednesday 'client visits' that conveniently covered shooting practice. "I'll need copies of those records."

"Sure thing." Rick hesitated. "This guy do something bad?"

Jake tucked the photos away. "His marksmanship training wasn't for corporate security."

As Rick photocopied the appointment pages, Jake stared through reinforced glass at the practice range. Kyle had spent months preparing for murder, using business trips as cover while Anna sat home unknowing.

His phone buzzed with a text from Katherine. "Found Anna's alibi witnesses. Kyle acted alone. Where are you?"

Jake typed back: "Richmond. Kyle's been practicing."

Katherine stood at the whiteboard in the precinct conference room, marker in hand. Detective Eden sat across from Margaret, with Sammi taking notes from the other end.

"Kyle was already inside when Misty brought James to the museum," Katherine began, drawing a simple floor plan. "Hiding in the service corridor near the new exhibit hall, probably with remote access to the monitors so he could see what was happening. His wife doesn't give him enough credit. It took some serious intelligence to put this together." She marked an X on the diagram. "Misty brings James into the exhibit."

"How did he know that she would leave?" Margaret asked.

"That was dumb luck. But he could have gotten her out of the room with a phone call in the service area."

"Then what?" Eden chimed in.

"When she left, he disabled camera twelve, stepped into the room and whacks James over the head. He lowered him to the ground and put a patch of fake blood on the floor."

"Fake blood?" Eden and Margaret almost simultaneously.

"He had plastic sheeting and paint at his house, remember? He just had to cover a sheet with dark paint and cut it into the shape of a blood pool."

"That would never fool anyone," Sammi interjected.

"But it didn't have to fool the police, just an excitable wife who knows that she could be blamed for the murder," Katherine replied. "Misty told me that she saw the body in the middle of the room. *But she didn't see the wound.* After Misty left, Kyle repositioned James's unconscious body under the display table and shot him. That's why there was no blood trail."

"What if Misty had called 911?" Margaret asked.

"Remember that Kyle knew a lot about Misty's psychology. He heard her secrets from Anna. He knows she is excitable and apt to overreact about things. Even if she had called 911, he would have had time to commit the murder and hide before emergency responders arrived." Katherine capped the marker. "That's why Misty didn't hear the gunshot. She was already gone. Then he just pulled the wires of camera twelve as he left to make it look like an amateur job."

Eden shook her head slowly. "And his alibi?"

"Timer switches, call forwarding, and duct tape." Katherine winked at Sammi. "We've already tested how that works."

"And using Gavin's identity at the museum, he had the perfect setup," Margaret said.

"*Almost* perfect," Katherine corrected. "He forgot about the cash transactions in Richmond."

35

Katherine and Detective Eden walked across the SecureTech Solutions parking lot, their breath visible in the January air.

"Feels good to get this right," Rhonda said, checking her radio. "Backup's in position around the building."

"Thirty years of jealousy," Katherine mused, looking up at the modern glass facade. "Kyle's been planning this for longer than we thought. Maybe not the specific details, but the resentment? That's been festering since high school."

"Think he'll run?"

"No. He's too arrogant. Probably thinks he can still talk his way out of this." Katherine pulled open the door. "People like Kyle always believe they're the smartest person in the room."

The receptionist looked up nervously as they approached. "Can I help you?"

"Police. We need to speak with Kyle Bovill," Rhonda said, showing her badge.

"He's in his office. Should I call—"

"No need." Katherine headed for the stairs.

They found Kyle in his corner office on a conference call, his back to the door.

"—So the encryption protocols need to be updated across all client systems, correct? We can't have another vulnerability like—" Kyle spun around as they entered, his eyes widening. "I'll have to call you back." He hung up and threw out his arms. "Detective Eden! And Ms. Carson! What brings you here? Is this about Anna? Because I've been trying to reach her lawyer, but—"

"Kyle Bovill," Eden interrupted, pulling out handcuffs, "you're under arrest for the murders of James Vanderlin and Beth Taylor."

Kyle's face went white. "Murders? This is completely ridiculous! Why would I—I mean, what possible reason could I have? James was my friend!"

"Turn around and put your hands behind your back," Eden ordered.

"I—the thing is," Kyle's confidence cracked as she cuffed him, "James and I were close. Ask anyone! We worked together for years!"

Other employees had gathered in the hallway, drawn by the commotion. Kyle's face flushed red with embarrassment.

"You have the right to remain silent," Eden began.

"This is a mistake! I demand to know what evidence you think you have! You can't just arrest someone without proof!"

An hour later, Kyle sat in Interview Room 2 at Baltimore PD, hands motioning frantically even while cuffed to the table.

Katherine leaned back in her chair, studying him. "Was James really your friend?"

"We were close! Anyone can tell you that! I helped him with everything. Security systems, client presentations, technical problems."

"We spoke to your employees," Eden stated flatly. "They said you constantly tried to one-up him. Always had to be the expert in the room."

Kyle's hands fluttered nervously. "That's just healthy competition! Everyone does that in business! You have to stay sharp, keep your edge. James understood that!"

"Not everyone murders their competition." Katherine slid crime scene photos across the table. "Your first kill was almost perfect. Professional, calculated. But Beth Taylor?" She tapped the second set of images. "Sloppy. Rushed. What happened?"

"I don't know what you're talking about! Why would I hurt Beth? She was just the assistant curator! I barely knew her!"

"She saw you at the museum," Katherine interrupted. "Probably thought nothing of it at first. But after our conversation about the offline camera, she started thinking. Who would know how to disable camera twelve?"

Kyle went pale, his gestures suddenly still. "You can't prove— I mean, lots of people have access to—"

"The person who installed it," Eden finished. "Beth knew it wasn't Gavin Tucker. She knew you from the events you and Anna attended with the Vanderlins."

"This is all circumstantial! You have no evidence! Correct? You're just fishing, hoping I'll say something incriminating!"

"Richmond Precision Point Shooting Range," Katherine said calmly. "Tuesday and Wednesday training sessions. Cash payments for advanced marksmanship. Want to explain those business trips, Kyle?"

Kyle's expression froze. "I—well—those were legitimate client meetings in the Richmond area. I can show you the invoices—"

"Eleanor Abernathy identified you as the camera installer," Katherine interrupted.

"And we have a statement from Gavin Tucker," Rhonda added, "proving how you rigged your alibi. Why did you kill Beth? She figured it out, didn't she?"

Kyle stared at the table, his hands finally still. The silence lingering for nearly a minute before he looked up, speaking softly.

"She called me Friday afternoon. Said she'd been thinking about your conversation, about the cameras being offline during the murder. Asked what I knew about the installation."

"And?"

"I told her Gavin handled all the museum work, but she said that was funny because she saw me at the museum." Kyle's shoulders sagged. "She was putting it together. The offline camera, the timing, my access to the security system."

Katherine nodded. "You arranged to meet her."

"I tried to convince her she was wrong! I explained that multiple people had access, that it could have been anyone! But she kept asking questions, kept pushing." Kyle's voice rose, his hands moving wildly again. "You called while I was with her. After she hung up, she turned to me with this look—like she'd just won the lottery. Said now she had leverage. That she could tell you everything she knew about me being at the museum, or ..." Kyle's voice cracked. "Or we could come to an arrangement."

"She was trying to blackmail you."

"She said she knew I'd killed James, and she had evidence. When you called asking about guns, she saw her opportunity. Put on that helpful act to scare me, show me how easily she could destroy everything." His hands shook.

"So you shot her."

"She was going to ruin everything! Anna would find out what I'd done, the police would investigate deeper ... The FBI was already sniffing around Anna. I thought if I framed Misty perfectly, they'd close the murder case and focus on their espionage charges. Two birds, one stone. Otherwise, all of it—thirty years of waiting for the perfect opportunity—would be for nothing!"

"Thirty years?" Rhonda raised an eyebrow.

Kyle laughed bitterly, his professional mask vanishing. "You think this just happened? Oh! Oh my! You have no idea how long I've been planning this. I've been watching him succeed for thirty years while I stayed in the background. James took everything from me. Anna chose him first, remember? Back in high school, she was mine until James decided he wanted her too."

"You decided to take it all away from him."

"Correct." Kyle straightened, some of his old arrogance returning. "And I almost succeeded. The perfect crime, the perfect frame job. It had to be perfect. Just killing James wasn't enough. Any idiot with a gun could do that. I needed to destroy them both, and I needed them to know I was smarter than they ever gave me credit for. If Beth had just minded her own business and kept her mouth shut ..."

Katherine and Rhonda exchanged glances. Kyle Bovill had just confessed to double murder, his thirty-year obsession finally consuming him.

36

The heavy door of Baltimore Central Booking clanged shut behind Misty Vanderlin as she stepped into the late afternoon sunlight. She looked pale and disoriented, clutching a small bag of personal items, her dark hair pulled back in a simple ponytail.

Margaret waited by the steps, arms open. "Oh, hon, come here."

Misty fell into her college friend's embrace, her shoulders shaking. "Margaret, I can't believe this is over. I thought—I really thought—"

"Shh. It's finished. You're free." Margaret held her tightly. "The charges are completely dropped."

Katherine approached more cautiously, hands in her coat pockets. Misty looked up and immediately reached for her.

"Katherine, thank you. Thank you so much." Misty's hug was fierce, desperate. "Margaret told me everything you did to prove my innocence."

"I'm just glad we got to the truth," Katherine said.

Misty stepped back, wiping her eyes. "I still can't process it. Kyle? Kyle killed James?" She shook her head. "He was always intense, competitive, but murder?"

"Complete confession," Katherine confirmed. "Once we laid out the evidence—the shooting range training, the camera sabotage, Eleanor's identification—he broke down. Thirty years of jealousy finally came out."

"And Anna was selling company secrets this whole time?"

Margaret guided them toward her car. "People hide things, Misty. Even from those they work with daily."

"The FBI has taken Anna into custody," Katherine noted. "Corporate espionage carries serious federal charges."

Misty stared out the window as they pulled away from the jail. "You remember what you told me before? About finding out who I am without James?"

Katherine nodded. "You said you'd been half of a couple since college."

"I've been thinking about it every day in that cell." Misty's voice grew stronger. "Maybe this horrible experience—as awful as it sounds—maybe it's forcing me to finally figure out who Misty Vanderlin really is."

"It doesn't sound awful," Katherine said gently. "It sounds like survival."

"The prosecutor, Mr. Griffith, seemed so certain I was guilty."

"Kyle planned it that way," Margaret stated. "Your gun, your presence at the scene, the text from your phone. He orchestrated everything to frame you."

Misty closed her eyes, leaning back against the headrest. "I keep thinking about that night. If I'd stayed, if I'd called 911 instead of running—"

"Kyle would have killed you too," Katherine said firmly. "He could have made it look like a murder suicide or staged your disappearance to look like guilt. Running saved your life."

As they turned onto Misty's street, she looked up at her house—the home she'd shared with James, where Kyle had stolen her gun from the safe.

"I don't think I can stay here," she whispered.

"Then don't," Margaret replied. "You can stay with me as long as you need."

Misty turned to face Katherine. "Will you come to James's memorial service? When we reschedule it, now that his name is cleared?"

"Of course."

"Thank you. Both of you." Misty's voice was steadier now. "For believing in me when I could barely believe in myself."

37

Pizza boxes covered the coffee table at the Carson Investigations office, and Lee had broken out a bottle of champagne from his desk drawer. Sammi was recounting her successful interrogation of Gavin for the third time, gesturing animatedly with a slice of pepperoni.

"And when I mentioned James Vanderlin, his whole face just changed. You could see the fear, but also relief that he could finally tell someone what Kyle had been up to."

"First solo interview and you cracked the case wide open." Jake raised his glass. "Not bad for a rookie."

Katherine smiled, feeling the tension of the past weeks finally lifting. "Kyle's confession ties everything together. Misty's free, Anna's facing federal charges, and—"

Her phone buzzed. Unknown number. She almost ignored it, then reconsidered. "Katherine Carson."

"Ms. Carson? This is Cynthia. Christopher's girlfriend ..."

Katherine straightened, the celebration fading. "What's wrong, Cynthia?"

"Another meeting. Tonight. Chris is nervous, keeps checking his watch. He left twenty minutes ago with a briefcase full of cash."

Katherine grabbed a pen. "Where?"

"Same as before. Pier Seven at Harbor East. He said to expect him back late."

"Thank you. Stay safe, Cynthia."

Katherine hung up and looked at Jake. "Euler's making another drop tonight."

Jake was already reaching for his jacket.

"But we just closed a double homicide. Can't this wait?" Sammi asked.

"The money laundering connects to something bigger. We've seen organized crime elements, professional security. This could be our chance to understand the full scope."

Lee looked up from his champagne. "Y'all want backup?"

"No. Too many people will spook them." Katherine checked her weapon. "Jake and I can handle surveillance."

"Save us some pizza," Jake said. "We'll be back."

An hour later, Katherine and Jake sat in a car across from Pier Seven, watching Christopher Euler pace nervously beside his Honda. The briefcase sat on his trunk, and he checked his phone every few seconds.

"There," Jake pointed to a black SUV approaching. "Same vehicle from Maritime Solutions."

Quinn Pham emerged from the SUV, scanning the area with professional caution. The exchange was swift. Briefcase for a manila envelope. But this time, instead of leaving separately, they drove off in the same direction.

"Follow the SUV," Katherine instructed.

Jake started the engine, keeping well back as they tracked the vehicle through downtown Baltimore. The SUV turned into the warehouse district, finally stopping at a loading dock behind a faded building.

"Industrial Arts Storage," Katherine read from the sign. "Private warehouse facility."

They parked in the shadows between two shipping containers and watched Quinn Pham exit his vehicle. He walked to a side entrance where another figure waited in the doorway.

Katherine raised her binoculars and froze. "Jake. Look."

Jake focused his own binoculars on the waiting figure. "That's Paul Zabala."

The museum shipping manager stepped forward to greet Quinn Pham, and they disappeared inside together.

"Zabala's suspicious quarterly bonuses," Katherine said in a low voice. "Not performance payments. Laundering fees."

"Makes sense. Museum shipping operations would be the perfect cover. International shipments, established customs relationships, legitimate paperwork."

"And Zabala had access to insider information. He knew about the exhibit schedules, security changes, everything." Katherine lowered her binoculars.

"Think Paul knew about Kyle's plan?"

"No. Kyle was focused on framing Misty. But this operation gave Kyle additional cover; another reason for suspicious activity around the museum."

Jake started the car as the warehouse lights went out. "Two separate crimes, same location. No wonder this case felt so complex."

"We need the FBI. This is bigger than local money laundering." Katherine pulled out her phone. "Agent Chen needs to know about Zabala's involvement."

38

Paul Zabala looked up from his computer as Katherine, Jake, and Agent Chen entered the museum's shipping department, three federal agents positioned by the exits.

"FBI," Chen announced, showing his badge. "We need to discuss your business relationship with Quinn Pham."

Zabala's eyes darted toward the loading dock, but Jake had already moved to block that exit. "I think you should stay and chat."

"What's this about?" Zabala demanded, his voice strained.

Katherine crossed her arms. "Quarterly bonuses of twenty-five hundred dollars. Industrial Arts Storage. A known art smuggler. Ring any bells?"

Zabala looked back and forth between Katherine and Chen. "I don't know what you're talking about."

"We followed Pham to your meeting last night," Katherine said. "We have photographs."

Zabala's shoulders sagged. "You don't understand the whole situation."

"Then explain it." Katherine said, settling into a chair. "Help us understand."

"The bonuses, yes, they're payments. But I only handle the shipping arrangements." Zabala looked at Katherine, then quickly away.

"You have a partner," Katherine stated, her mind racing to assemble the pieces. "Who? Someone else at the museum?"

Zabala shook his head firmly. "I won't give you a name."

"This partner of yours—they have the same payment pattern you do?"

Zabala's silence was telling.

"They've been receiving identical quarterly payments," Katherine continued. "Someone with access to museum authentication procedures."

"I'm not saying anything more about my partner's identity," Zabala said firmly.

"But they handled the sophisticated part—the forgeries, the documentation, the museum credentials."

Chen leaned towards the suspect. "Zabala, you're looking at serious federal charges. Cooperation might—"

"No." Zabala's voice was resolute. "I won't name names. My partner ... they don't deserve to go down for this."

"For stealing art from the museum?" Katherine raised an eyebrow.

"No," Zabala groaned. "We only ever sell forgeries."

Jake walked closer. "So you're protecting someone who's been using museum resources to authenticate forged art?"

"We protected the museum too," Zabala shot back defensively. "No forged pieces were ever exhibited. Kept the museum's reputation intact."

Katherine studied Zabala's face, reading the loyalty and protectiveness there. "That warehouse accident, you caused it."

Zabala nodded. "When you started looking at shipping records, I knew you'd eventually find the payment patterns."

"But we kept investigating anyway," Katherine remarked. "You didn't cause that accident to protect this operation. You did it to protect your partner."

Zabala's head snapped up. He opened his mouth as if to respond, but didn't say anything.

Agent Chen stepped forward. "Paul Zabala, you're under arrest for conspiracy to commit art fraud and money laundering."

As the agents moved in, Zabala looked directly at Katherine. "My partner and I had nothing to do with the murders. Whatever else they're involved in, they're not violent."

As they led Zabala away, Agent Chen turned to Katherine. "Director Irvine mentioned he'd made you an offer to work undercover on the Euler case. You should consider it. We could use someone with your instincts tracking financial crimes."

Jake stared at Agent Chen. "Did you just give Katherine a compliment?"

"I acknowledged good police work," Chen replied stiffly.

Katherine watched through the window as Zabala was placed in the federal vehicle, still protecting someone whose identity was now glaringly obvious to her.

"Well," Jake said, "at least we know there's another player in this art fraud."

"Yes," Katherine replied thoughtfully. "We do."

39

Katherine found them in Margaret's living room, tea cups on the table between them, both women laughing at some shared memory from college.

Margaret waved at her with a warm smile. "Come in, hon. We were just catching up."

Misty looked up from the couch, her face still bright with laughter. "Katherine, thank you for everything. I feel like I'm finally starting to breathe again."

Katherine remained standing, her expression carefully neutral. "I have news about the Botticelli sketch. The results came back from the Swiss lab."

"And?" Misty asked, leaning forward.

"It's authentic. Genuine Renaissance work, just as you determined."

Misty smiled with satisfaction. "I knew it would be. I did all the authentication work myself before the acquisition."

Margaret poured Katherine a cup of tea. "Then why was James so convinced it was fake? He seemed obsessed with proving something was wrong with it."

Katherine accepted the coffee but didn't sit down. "Because Beth Taylor believed it was fake."

"Beth?" Misty frowned. "But she accepted the authentication eventually."

"She did. But initially, she believed it was fraudulent because someone had tried to recruit her into an art forgery operation." Katherine's voice remained steady, professional. "When she realized the Botticelli was actually genuine, she tried to get James to drop his investigation. But he wouldn't."

Margaret set down her cup. "What kind of operation?"

"Sophisticated art fraud. Using museum credentials to authenticate forged pieces, creating false provenance for stolen artwork. The kind of operation that requires someone with legitimate museum authority."

Misty shifted uncomfortably. "That's terrible. Thank goodness James was trying to stop it."

"If Kyle hadn't murdered him, James would likely have met the same fate," Katherine said quietly.

Margaret looked shocked. "How can you say that? You think these art criminals would have killed James?"

Katherine's expression hardened, her voice becoming stern and measured. "Yes, Margaret. I do think that. Because the person running the operation had too much to lose if James exposed her."

Katherine leveled her gaze at Misty. The woman's smile faded.

"The quarterly bonuses. Twenty-five hundred dollars every three months. The same payment schedule Paul Zabala was receiving."

Misty went stock still. "They were museum grants."

"No, they weren't. They were payments for authenticating forged artwork and stolen pieces. Paul confirmed it during his interrogation. He refused to name his partner, but the financial records tell the whole story."

Margaret looked between them, confusion written across her face. "Katherine, what are you saying?"

Katherine didn't take her eyes off the guilty woman. "I'm saying Misty Vanderlin has been running an art fraud operation through the Walters Museum for years. Using her position as curator to provide legitimate authentication for stolen and forged pieces."

"That's ridiculous!" Misty stood up abruptly. "I would never—"

"You recruited Beth Taylor," Katherine continued relentlessly. "When she refused to participate, you had to be more careful. But James started investigating Beth's concerns, and that threatened everything you'd built."

Misty's face went pale. "You can't prove any of this."

"Paul's cooperation. Financial records. The payment patterns. Your access to authentication procedures." Katherine's voice remained calm. "It's over, Misty."

Margaret stared at her college friend in horror. "Misty? Tell me this isn't true."

Misty looked between them, her composure finally cracking. "You don't understand. The museum needed the money. Funding was being cut, important acquisitions were being lost to other institutions. I was helping preserve art history."

"By stealing it," Katherine said flatly.

"By finding new homes for pieces that were sitting in private collections, unseen by the public!" Misty's voice rose. "Yes, some of the paperwork was ... creative. But the art was real, the preservation was legitimate!"

Margaret sank back into her chair. "Oh, Misty!"

Katherine walked to the window and gestured outside. "Agent Chen is waiting in the car. He has a federal warrant for your arrest."

Margaret looked up at Katherine with tears in her eyes. "She just got out of jail for murder charges. Now this?"

"I'm sorry, Margaret." Katherine walked to the door and opened it. Agent Chen was already walking up the path.

"Misty Vanderlin," Chen began as he entered, "you're under arrest for conspiracy to commit art fraud, money laundering, and trafficking in stolen goods."

As the cuffs clicked into place, Misty looked at Margaret one last time. "I never meant for anyone to get hurt. I was trying to save art, not destroy lives."

Margaret couldn't meet her eyes. "How could you let me defend you, knowing you were guilty of this?"

"I wasn't guilty of murder," Misty responded. "That part was real."

As Agent Chen led her away, Katherine sat down beside Margaret, who was staring at her hands.

"I vouched for her," Margaret whispered. "I staked my reputation on her innocence."

"You believed in your friend. That's not a crime."

"But I was so wrong about who she really was."

Katherine nodded. "Sometimes the people we think we know best are the ones hiding the most secrets."

"But I was so wrong about who she really was." Margaret's voice cracked. She collapsed into Katherine's arms, sobbing. It was as if all the stress and exhaustion of the past week came crashing over her. "I believed in her! I told everyone she was innocent, that she was just a grieving widow trying to find herself!" Her words came out between gasps. "And all along, she was a criminal. All that talk about discovering who she was without James—she already knew exactly who she was. A fraud."

Katherine stroked Margaret's hair, letting her cry. Outside, a car door slammed, and Misty Vanderlin disappeared into federal custody.

People wear masks, Katherine thought as she comforted her friend. *Some to hide from trauma, some to hide from truth, and some to hide their crimes.* The hardest lesson she'd learned since Daniel's death was that healing meant removing all the masks. Even the ones that protect you from pain.

Katherine sat alone on her apartment balcony, staring out at the Baltimore skyline. The evening was warm for January, and the city hummed quietly below. She'd been sitting there for an hour, processing the events of the past week, when she heard her apartment door open.

"Katie?" Jake's voice called from inside.

"Out here," she replied.

Jake appeared in the doorway, his face creased with concern. "Saw the news about Misty." He studied her carefully. "How are you holding up?"

Katherine gestured to the chair beside her. "I'm okay, really."

Jake settled into the deck chair. "How's Margaret taking it?"

"About as well as you'd expect. Having your college friend turn out to be a criminal mastermind isn't easy to process."

Jake nodded. "You did good work, Katie. That interrogation with Zabala, the way you pieced together Misty's involvement, getting a compliment from Chen ... " They both chuckled at that.

"Daniel used to say I had good instincts," Katherine said. "Not because of the training, but in spite of it. Maybe he was right. Maybe I've been trusting the wrong voice all these years."

Jake leaned forward in his chair. "Katie, I've watched you work. The best insights you have, the connections you make don't come from protocol. They come from instinct. From caring about the truth." He spoke with conviction. "That's not training. That's you."

The stars blurred slightly as her eyes filled with unexpected tears, but for the first time since Daniel's death, they weren't tears of grief. They were tears of gratitude for second chances, for friends who became family, and for the quiet satisfaction of work that mattered.

Two Weeks Later ...

"We've lost the Rothschild necklace!"

Maya Garcia stared at the empty velvet slot in the vault's most secure display case. The $1.1 million art deco masterpiece that had been locked behind three layers of security just yesterday was missing.

"Thomas, when was the last time you saw it?" Maya's voice stayed calm even as her mind raced through protocols. Nine years in the jewelry business, the last three as Radcliffe's Director of Operations and Inventory, had taught her that panic solved nothing. But missing inventory worth more than most people's houses? That could destroy them.

"Yesterday afternoon," Thomas stammered, his face pale. "Mrs. Whitmore looked at it around four, but she decided on the emerald suite instead."

Maya hurried to the back office computer, her fingers flying across the keyboard as she pulled up the security logs. Camera angles, entry codes, motion sensor data—everything had to be accounted for before she called the insurance company. One missing piece could trigger a full audit, bring media attention, and shatter customer confidence.

The Dell monitor flickered as she scrolled through the digital records. "There," she breathed, relief flooding through her. "Display case seven in the main showroom. Someone moved it yesterday for a client viewing and forgot to return it to the vault."

The tension in the back room evaporated as Thomas sagged against the wall. "Thank goodness. I thought we'd been robbed."

"Never assume theft before you check human error," Maya said, making a note to retrain the evening staff on vault protocols. "And Thomas? Next time, double-check before you give me a heart attack."

Her phone buzzed with a text from her husband Carlos: *Sammi's working late again. That detective agency keeps her busy!*

Maya smiled, thinking of her niece hunched over case files, probably surviving on takeout and determination. Last night at dinner, Sammi had been bubbling with excitement about some surprise party she was planning—something about pink decorations and handmade flowers.

"Maya, the morning deposits are ready," Janet called from the front.

"Perfect. And make sure the Rothschild goes back in vault position A-7 before—"

The front door burst open.

Two men in dark suits strode in with a kind of purposeful momentum that made Maya's blood freeze. Federal agents. She knew the walk, the way they scanned the room, cataloging exits and witnesses before their targets even knew they were being hunted.

The taller one's eyes locked on hers across the fine jewelry showroom. "Maya Garcia?"

Time slowed. The elegant display cases suddenly felt like prison walls. Customers browsing engagement rings became unwitting audience members to her nightmare.

"Yes?" The word came out like a squeak.

"Immigration and Customs Enforcement. We need to discuss your documentation."

Maya's clipboard slipped from her fingers, clattering onto the marble floor. Around her, the store's morning bustle died and conversations stopped mid-sentence.

"There's been some mistake," Maya said, her voice steadier than she felt.

The agent smiled, but it never reached his eyes. "Ma'am, there's no mistake. Someone's provided us with very compelling evidence about irregularities in your immigration status."

Maya's world tilted. The life she'd built—the systems she'd perfected, the reputation she'd earned, the family who trusted her—all of it balanced on a knife's edge.

Someone had done this deliberately. Someone wanted her destroyed.

And as the second agent moved to block the exit, Maya realized with crystal clarity that her carefully ordered life was about to explode.

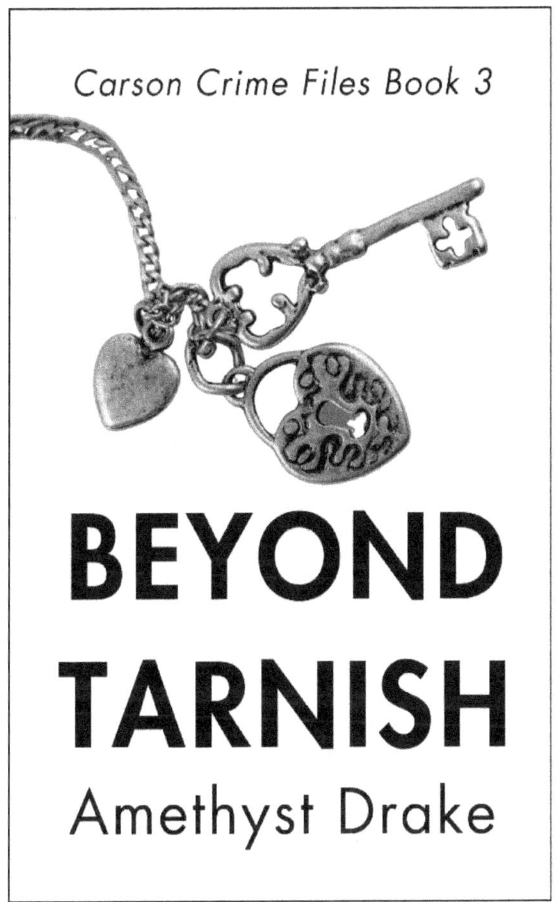

Coming January 2026

**Subscribe to my Newsletter at
AmethystDrake.com**

About the Walters Art Museum

If you enjoyed following Katherine Carson through the halls of the Walters Art Museum in *Framed*, you'll be delighted to know this Baltimore treasure is very real and even more impressive than fiction!

The museum exists because Henry Walters couldn't bear to see his family's life work locked away after his death in 1931. The collection started decades earlier with his father William T. Walters, but Henry transformed it into something extraordinary before making the bold decision to give it all—the entire art collection, two buildings, and enough money to keep the lights on—to the City of Baltimore with the simple but powerful mission that it serve "for the benefit of the public."

Today the museum houses more than 36,000 objects spanning 7,000 years of human creativity. The collection includes works by Monet, Manet, and other masters, plus some of the world's finest examples of decorative arts.

Here's the best part: admission to the Walters is completely free. The museum offers everything from ancient artifacts to contemporary art, plus a café and gift shop. And unlike Katherine's investigation, no suspicious security malfunctions or falling crates to worry about. The museum works to make art accessible to everyone, creating a place where you can spend hours discovering treasures from cultures around the world.

The Baroque gallery where James Vanderlin met his fictional demise? That's inspired by real spaces throughout the museum where Renaissance and Baroque masterpieces are displayed in intimate, atmospheric settings. And the central painting of this fictional exhibit, *Judith Decapitating Holofernes*, has actually been in the museum's permanent collection since the original 1931 bequest. But when I saw the massive oil on canvas for the first time, I thought, "This would be a good place for a murder."

Located in Baltimore's elegant Mount Vernon neighborhood, the museum occupies several historic buildings around the first monument built to honor George Washington. The main gallery, with its soaring sculpture court and palazzo architecture, provides a dramatic backdrop worthy of any mystery novel.

The Walters Art Museum is located at
600 North Charles Street in Baltimore.
For current exhibitions and hours, visit thewalters.org.

Did you enjoy *Framed?*

Please review!

A star rating and a sentence or two is the best thing you can do to support me.

Please consider rating and review on these popular book review sites and other retailers.

The StoryGraph

Goodreads

Amazon

Barnes and Noble

Anywhere books are sold!

About the Author

Amethyst Drake is a passionate storyteller. She excels at crafting delightful characters and enjoys developing com-plex relationships among them. Mystery has always been her favorite genre to read, making it a natural choice for her writing. She aims to blend her personal experience with mental health and the moral complexities of intricate interpersonal relationships into engaging novels.

Her first novel, *The Scheme,* has been awarded the presti-gious indie B.R.A.G. Medallion, recognizing outstanding quality and impact on readers worldwide. This honor places it among a select group of reader-recommended, independently published books at the Book Readers Appreciation Group (BRAG).

Amethyst loves reading all kinds of mysteries, suspense, and thrillers and enjoys watching classic detective and espionage dramas like "Murder, She Wrote," "Perry Mason," and "Mission: Impossible." She also loves hearing from readers! Connect by signing up for her newsletter at amethystdrake.com or email amethyst@agswordsmiths.com.

www.ingramcontent.com/pod-product-compliance
Lightning Source LLC
Chambersburg PA
CBHW070503300726
48975CB00007B/2296